EVIE MITCHELL

Wrath

Book 2 | Nameless Souls MC

Contents

Connect with Evie Mitchell

Website
www.EvieMitchell.com

Instagram, Facebook and TikTok
@EvieMitchellAuthor

Facebook Group
Evie Mitchell's Greedy Reader Book Club

Books by Evie Mitchell

Nameless Souls MC Series
Runner
Wrath
Ghost

Elliot Security Series
Rough Edge
Bleeding Edge
Knife Edge

Capricorn Cove Series
Thunder Thighs
Double the D
Muffin Top
The Mrs. Clause
Beach Party
New Year Knew You
The Shake-Up
Double Breasted
As You Wish
You Sleigh Me
Resolution Revolution
Meat Load
Trunk Junk (Coming soon)

Archer Sibling Series
Just Joshing

Dedication

As always to my husband,
the only man I'd allow in my end of days shelter.
And only because you give me the good D.

To Liz Netz,
who is going to be the best goddamned nurse alive.
Girl, I am so fucking proud of you!

Wrath

Wrath

Five years ago, I walked away from the woman I loved.
She told me she loved another.
She lied.
In the before she had protections.
In the after? I am her protection.
And there's nothing that'll keep me from taking what's mine.

Trigger warning: This is a darker series than my other books and contains some violence. Happily ever afters are still guaranteed, but this is a gritty series so proceeded with caution.

The Story So Far

Day 463 – Post the dark

I'm not really sure what to write in this history of the after. It feels more like confessional than a factual retelling.

The virus came quickly, ravaging its way across the world—disproportionately affecting the female population. Borders closed, as governments panicked, attempting to stop the spread of the infection.

For a while it seemed like they had succeeded and a vaccine was only weeks away. Then the cities began to go dark. Fragments of news about a mutation reaching us before society faded away leaving every man and woman to simply fight for survival.

The world as we knew it had officially ended.

A year before the dark, I'd been approached by Audrey to join a ragtag group of women who were planning to see out the after at our University. With no other choices, I'd agreed—lending my expert knowledge of botany to their team.

There had been thirteen of us, all with speciality skillsets, each bringing something unique and useful to the table. We'd worked well, building a safe space, a home in the after.

Then The Purge ripped our sense of safety away, stealing two of our members along with them. The militia attracted a certain type of man who saw women as nothing but commodities.

Knowing our haven was no longer viable, we scrambled to find an alternative option. Which led me to my past—the Nameless Souls Motorcycle Club.

We'd approached the club offering them our skills in exchange for protection. They'd agreed when Ellie had presented them with an offer they couldn't refuse—biofuel.

Now we were on a mission to take this knowledge to the other chapters, bringing them hope where before there had been none.

Or at least that was the plan. God help us.

Prologue

Wrath

I tipped the beer back, taking a sip as I watched Kate stumble her way back to the bar. Her cheeks were flushed, her eyes glassy.

She's drunk.

She tripped, stumbling into me, laughing as I caught her.

"Thanks." She twisted out of my arms, slapping a hand on the bar. "Another, milady!"

"You're drunk," I remarked.

"Yee-ep." She smacked her lips together, emphasizing the p, then reached for the shot Kimi placed before her.

I shot Kimi a questioning look. She shook her head, placing a hand on her pregnant belly.

Kate lifted the shot glass, holding it at mouth level.

"I'm drunk as a skunk in a… in a…." She frowned, dropping her arm as she tried to work out what rhymed with skunk. "Punk? Bunk? Monk?" She slapped her free hand on the bar then pointed it at me, yelling, "Drunk as a skunk!"

She tipped the shot, downing it in one, then slammed the glass on the bar and looked over at Kimi.

"Another?" Kimi asked, her right eyebrow lifted in question.

"A cider, my lady." Kate burped then giggled, twirling on the barstool to look up at me. "Where were we?"

I raised one eyebrow. "Nowhere? You just sat down."

She waved her hand dismissively. "Nah, we were talking about something."

Like how I'm about to cut you off and force you to go sleep this bender off?

"That's right!" She leaned towards me, nearly slipping off her seat. My arm shot out, steadying her. She sent me a grateful look, patting my hand in thanks.

I ignored the way that made my cock harden. I was used to ignoring that reaction around Kate.

"I was asking why you motorcycle people have an obsession with death and hell and sup-a-nat-a-ru-al"—the word sounded not quite right coming out of her mouth but she pushed through—"beings. Like hell and the devils and grim reapers and shit. You know what's scary?"

She narrowed her eyes on me, leaning close. "Raptors."

"Raptors?" I asked, ignoring the chuckles from the crowd around us. Kate never got drunk. Hell, she'd declared she wouldn't be drinking until her university graduation—and that was still a fair ways off.

She nodded her head earnestly. "Raptors. That shit is *terrifying.*"

Kimi handed her another drink and she decided to use her mouth to pick it up and chug it rather than her hands. Impressively, she managed to get a quarter of the bottle down before air became a requirement.

Fuck.

I shifted, subtly adjusting my crotch. Kate dropped her head, the bottle falling to the bar but miraculously remaining upright, her hands still on her legs. The crowd whistled and catcalled, and I made a mental note of who I needed to fuck up later.

Kate reached out, touching my arm, and recapturing my attention, continuing her rant.

"Raptors. I have doorknobs all over my house. Not handles. You know why? 'Cause they *learn*. They *learn* shit, Wrath. They know how to open doors!" She swung her hands out, knocking my beer. I snatched it, righting the bottle.

"And once they know that, they can get to you and rip you open from here—" She lifted her shirt pointing at her belly button then dragged both her shirt and her finger up her body. "—to here." Her finger rested just under her collarbone; shirt bunched right up.

Fantastic breasts. Lace bra. God fucking help me.

I reached out, tugging her shirt down. "Pretty sure they're extinct."

"But people are trying to bring them back. It's genetic manipulation, Wrath. Terrifying."

"Did you watch *Jurassic Park* again?"

She shook her head, expression earnest. "Nah-uh. I read it. They want to try and do it. Bring shit that's extinct back. Danger-ous," she declared, slapping her hand against the bar. "They do that, before you know it, we'll be surrounded by zombies and ain't nobody got time for that."

My lips quirked up at the side and she grinned brightly at me before lifting my beer to her lips. "Just saying."

I watched her throat move as she swallowed. The images running through my head were definitely not kid-friendly.

Fuck you're a monster.

"You done yet?" I asked gruffly, wanting to get her home and safe.

She shook her head. "No. I'm gonna play pool." She swung around on the stool, beer still in hand, and stopped.

"Damn. Pope's using it." She tilted her head, squinting. "Is that Leslie? I thought she was banned after the last Gus-related incident"

Fucking Leslie. Seriously.

I glanced over, my normal *don't fuck with me* look back on my face. "She is."

"Well, Pope's doing her on the table." She hopped down. "I'll dance till they're done." She started moving to the jukebox.

I jerked my head at one of the prospects hovering nearby, nodding towards Leslie and Pope. He swallowed but nodded, heading over to break them up.

"What the fuck has gotten into her?" I asked Ice, who'd been sitting on the other side of me.

"Anniversary of her mum's death is today. It's been five years since she came to live with Gus." Ice lifted his beer to his lips, pausing as he glanced over at Kate. "She got her acceptance to Oxford today. Just like she and her mum planned. She was all set to go to the UK, study at that fancy-arse school." He shook his head. "Gus refused."

"Fuck."

Gus may have been a good chapter president, but the man was a fucking dick to his family. Cheated on his old lady (though rumour had it she encouraged it), had a troop of kids to different women—all of which he treated like shit.

I mean, one of his kids had rebelled by enlisting. Straight as a fucking line, that one.

Kate was the only daughter (that we knew of) in his brood. By all reports, her mother, Rumi, had been club pussy, only interested in partying and fucking, right up until Gus had knocked her up. Then she'd turned it around, becoming a killer single mum, working three jobs, and still managing to be home to tuck Kate into bed. The club respected her, though she'd never asked anything of us beyond asking Gus to have a relationship with Kate.

I'd been new to club life when Rumi'd been killed by a drunk driver. At just fourteen, Kate had moved in with Gus, and, for a little while, he'd seemed to grow a heart. It hadn't lasted beyond a month, and Mama, Gus' old lady, was more like the evil stepmother than a maternal figure.

I'd been a prospect back then, nineteen and angry at the world for dealing me a shit hand. But nothing had prepared me for the night I'd been told to escort Kate home from school. I'd arrived early, waiting out the front of the schoolyard, enjoying the looks the soccer mums threw my way—a mixture of morbid curiosity, fear, and attraction.

I may have flexed just for them.

When the bratty teens had gotten out, there'd been streams of them running out the gates, laughing and chatting, yelling goodbye, and promising to text later that night. In that sea, Kate had been an anomaly. She'd kept her head down, arms crossed tight over her chest as she flowed with the sea of movement but remained somehow apart from it.

I'd noted that not one person acknowledged her.

She'd clocked me early, the look on her face a mixture of relief and stoicism. She'd silently taken the helmet I'd offered her, pulling it on.

"Would have brought a cage if I'd known you weren't dressed for it." I apologized, nodding at her bare legs.

"It's fine," she'd told me, fiddling with the straps of her helmet.

"We don't have far to go."

I'd shrugged out of my jacket, handing it over to her. "At least wear this."

She'd taken it, offering me a small smile as she began to pull it on. She'd glanced behind me, her smile turning brittle, her movements pausing for a moment as she clocked the group behind me. I casually turned, glancing over as I swung a leg over my bike, settling into place.

The group had consisted of a couple of girls and a few guys. The guys had been making lewd gestures, the chicks giggling and whispering shit.

I pushed up my sunglasses, glaring. The girls had stopped first, immediately looking away. The guys had lasted a moment longer, ego and false pride not letting them give in. Finally, they'd shrugged, looking away, moving off.

House cats didn't mess with lions.

"Leave it." Kate swung onto my bike, wrapping her arms around me. "Just ignore them. They're small-minded idiots."

"They give you trouble often?"

"Nothing I can't handle."

I'd hated that she'd had to handle anything in the first place. I knew what it was like to be the kid others fucked over thinking they were hot shit.

I'd taken her home then told Gus I'd do the pick-up every afternoon. It'd started out innocently enough, me trying to give her a little slice of good. But it'd slowly changed. Kate had started hanging around the club gym where we all worked out. Then we'd turned those drives home into longer cruises, occasionally stopping for dinner or to visit her mother's grave.

At some point, over the last five years, I'd gone from thinking of her as the club's little sister to a woman I wanted to fuck.

And damn if that didn't make me a dirty fucker.

"He tell you?" Kimi asked, nodding at Ice.

"Yeah, Gus is a fucker." I glanced at our girl who was currently plugging in numbers on the jukebox. "No wonder she's looking to get fucked up."

Kate spun, shooting a grin at Ice as "Ice Ice Baby" pumped out over the loudspeakers. Every eye in the bar swung to the man beside me, laughter and catcalls following.

It was like a punch to my gut when she pointed at Ice, giving a little shimmy, inviting him onto the dance floor.

He shook his head, rolling his eyes but laughed as she began to sway, her hips swishing as she moved onto the small wooden dance floor, mouthing the lyrics at Ice.

She wiggled and ran hands over her body in an overly exaggerated manner, as if she were attempting to poke fun at dirty dancing before the white girl rap hand movements began. The boys laughed uproariously as she shuffled her way over to Ice's seat. Ice shut down; his face impassive as she swung her arse at him—drunk Kate could apparently twerk with the best of them.

She moved back out to the dance floor, finishing with an MC Hammer move, and taking a bow as wolf-whistles, cheers, and suggestions were thrown her way. Ice's face was stone cold, not a glint of humour in it, I expected mine was the same.

"I'm gonna go outside now," Kate declared, holding hands to her flushed cheeks.

"What?" Ice asked, but Kate had already turned, moving for the outdoor area.

I clapped a hand on his shoulder. "Stay, I got this."

I snatched up a jacket, knowing Kate would be cold as soon as she walked outside, and followed her happy skipping backside out into the yard.

Outside, in the frigid air, she swayed under the moon, arms wrapped around her middle as she moved to blend into the shadows of the Club House.

I came up behind her, draping the jacket over her shoulders. She sighed, leaning back against me.

"He said no, Wrath."

The mournful sorrow in her tone broke me. I wrapped my arms around her, pulling her back into me, dropping a kiss onto the crown of her hair. "I know, Sunshine. It's fucked."

She chuckled sadly, her breath catching. "It was going to be easy. I was going to pack up, leave. No regrets."

"What, none?"

She tilted her head back, giving me a sad smile. "Only that I'd miss you."

"Just me?"

God, I was a sick fuck.

She bit her lip, looking down. "Not just you."

"Who else?" I prompted, needing to have it confirmed.

"Ice," she whispered, her voice small. "I'll miss him as well."

Her words punched me in the gut, bitterness taking over. "You love him, don't you?"

Her breath caught, but she nodded, remaining silent.

I didn't say anything, just absorbed the blow.

"It doesn't matter now," she finally whispered into the quiet. "I know what I have to do."

The next day I went nomad, and when I next returned to the club, she was gone.

Chapter One

Kate

I was dreaming. I knew I was; I'd experienced this dream many times before. It was a flash between three separate memories. Some of the worst moments of my life.

The first was me at fourteen, being shoved down a set of concrete stairs at school. My body thumping loudly, pain exploding across my hips, back, shoulders, and thighs as I rolled to the bottom of the staircase. I'd picked myself up, tears streaming down my face, body screaming in pain. At the top of the staircase, arms crossed stood a boy, eyes cold and emotionless as he glared down at me.

"Guess I didn't push her hard enough. She's still walking." The people around him, the popular people, the ones who hung off his every word, chuckled nervously as they watched me scramble to collect my things. Something wet hit the side of my face. I'd reached for my cheek.

Spit.

Laughter came from the stairs.

"Get out of here, Kate. No one wants biker slut trash like you here." I'd scrambled, grabbing books, papers, and my backpack, and ran.

The dream moved ahead a few years. Prom. Blake Jimson had asked me. I was excited, thrilled. I'd worked overtime at my shitty waitressing job, scrimping, and saving for a dress. I'd known my mother, God rest her soul, would have wanted me to have this experience. Blake had picked me up at the end of my driveway. My dad, Gus, had been off doing something with the club. His old lady, Mama, hated me. I'd left with her yelling that if I'd got knocked up, I was out on my arse.

The plan had been to get dinner first, then head to the dance.

We'd never made it to dinner. Instead, he'd taken me to his girlfriend's house. I'd thought they were exes. A group of guys and girls had watched, laughing, as he'd pulled me out of the limo. In a flouncy jade dress and kitten heels, I'd been no match for him. He'd pulled me into the middle of her yard and proceeded to hold me down as each of the guys pissed on me. Five of them, one after another. Then they'd zipped their pants, grabbed their watching, laughing, dates, and taken the limo.

I'd assumed the driver had been paid off at some point, it was really the only reason any decent human wouldn't have helped me.

I'd sat on the curb. My phone in the clutch they'd tossed at me as they drove off. I'd pulled it out, debating who to call. Mama wouldn't give a shit. She'd tell me it was just what I'd deserved. Gus wouldn't answer my call, not if he was off doing club stuff. I called the prospects. Three of them arrived. Despite my asking for a car, they'd come on bikes. Stinking of piss, I'd mounted Wrath's ride. He hadn't complained. Hadn't said a word as I'd pressed my face into his shoulder and cried.

They'd taken me to the club gym, I'd washed and changed

into workout clothes from my locker and then strapped my hands. I'd exited the change rooms, starting to warm my body before heading for a punching bag.

"You want me to take you home?" Wrath had asked, icy fury in his gaze.

I'd shook my head, eyes on the bag not on the big boy-man beside me. "I'm good."

"Kate—"

"Gus said curfew was 1:00 a.m. I'm meant to be at dinner with Blake till seven then prom at seven thirty till whenever then afterparty. Then I'm meant to be home by 1:00 a.m. I am not going home until that time." I glanced up at him then back at the bag, pulling my hands up into sparring position. "They can't know about this."

"Why?"

I didn't answer, just started beating the shit out of the bag, determined to never be in that position again.

The dream shifted again, this time moving backward. Back to the night when my world ended.

I was home, dancing in my underwear, singing at the top of my lungs as I tidied the house. It was something I did regularly to help my mum. Underwear, old loose t-shirt, and the rocking tones of whatever band I felt in the mood for. The knock on the door was unexpected but not unwelcome. I threw it open with a grin expecting my mum, having forgotten her keys again. No one ever visited us, but we didn't mind.

"I didn't lock it you could have—" I stuttered to a stop. Face stricken, Ice stood in the doorway.

"Ice?"

"Kate." His voice was soft. "Let me in."

"Kate?" His voice sounded distant as I'd stared at him,

knowing. Knowing she was gone.

"Kate."

"No." My voice broke. "N-n-no. N-no, no, n-no, n-n-no!"

"Kate!"

I jerked up, pulling away from the hand on my arm. I rolled off the chair, hit the floor, and came up swinging.

"Whoa!" Ice held up his hands from his position on the hospital bed. "It's okay."

"Ice?" I shuddered, my eyes flicking from him to the room at large then back. "What?"

"You passed out." His lips quirked. "You should have gone home like I told you."

"Right." I dropped my hands, groaning as my back protested the slight movement. "God. My mouth tastes like arse."

"You know that for a fact?"

I raised my middle finger in reply.

He grinned, his ice-blue eyes watching me with an unsettling intensity.

"What?" I asked, running a hand through my hair. "Did I drool?"

"You're scared."

My stomach clenched but I pushed through, offering him a shrug, and settling back on the chair beside his bed. "Of course, I'm scared. You got hurt. We're leaving the safety of the compound. We have no idea what the next few months will look like."

I reached out, squeezing his hand. "And I'll miss you."

He snatched my hand, pulling me up and across the bed, crushing me to him. "You be careful, sis."

Sis. My insides warmed at the open acknowledgment that we were related. For years we'd had to hide the connection. Ice wouldn't have been safe if Gus had known he had another child. Instead, people had assumed we had some kind of interest in one another.

When I'd left, only Ice knew where I'd gone. Gus had set Ghost on my trail, but Ice had dealt with it, which had allowed me five blissful years of independence.

Returning to the club hadn't been easy. I knew I'd be making a sacrifice. I just hadn't realised how big a sacrifice that would be until now.

"You should go pack," he told me, his arms loosening around me. "Summer's coming but it's still cold and you're gonna be roughing it for a while."

I blinked back the tears stinging my eyes and nodded. "Okay."

"Don't cry, sis. You'll be fine, I'll recover, and we'll catch up when you return." He reached up, giving me a noogy. I pushed his hand away, laughing.

"Alright, I get the message. Don't hit on the nurse." I waggled a finger at him. "She deserves better than the likes of you."

"And yet Aella continues to touch me." Ice raised his hands linking them behind his head, grinning. "I'm just irresistible."

"Yep, must be that and not the hole in your leg." I leaned down, giving him one final hug. "I'll catch you later, brother."

"Be safe, Kate. Love you."

"Love you too." I pulled back, wiping at a stray tear. I immediately turned, heading for the door.

"Kate?"

I paused in the doorway, twisting to look at my brother. "Yeah?"

"Be kind to Wrath. He's been through a lot."

I nodded, biting my tongue.

"I'm serious, Kate. Since the world ended, he's seen shit. It's left a mark."

I paused; my tongue suddenly thick. "Okay, I'll try."

He nodded. "Thanks. And send Aella in when she's free. I think I need a sponge bath."

I laughed, flipping him the bird, and with one final look, I left.

Chapter Two

Kate

The forecourt of the compound bustled with activity. I watched, Switch and Zero, load the last of the gear into the back of a Wrangler. Off to one side, stood the rest of our travelling pack.

There was Ellie, our biochemist and the woman who'd created fuel from corn, and her man, Runner. They'd hooked up the night we'd arrived at the compound and had been joined at the hip ever since. Her fuel was the reason we were headed north, working our way up to the other Nameless Souls Motorcycle Club chapters. We were going to teach them how to make their own biofuel.

Beside them crouched Audrey, her long black hair pulled back into a ponytail. She had an open case on the ground and was pointing at the electronics inside. Pope stood over her, arms crossed as he made some comment that had her rolling her eyes. Audrey had designed her own mobile network which she was calling the 'A-Network'. The cases held the transmitters that would relay the signals from her readjusted mobile phones. If it worked—and it would because Audrey knew her shit—it would be the first type of communications between cities we'd had since the before.

Beyond them, Jo, our mechanic, and Texas stood in front of the two fuel tankers, playing scissors, paper, rock. Ava, our security specialist, and Ghost, the club's Sergeant at Arms, examined the retrofitted plating on the tankers, checking for weaknesses. Butcher and Lottie, the club's doctor, and our resident vet, rounded out our party.

Except for Wrath.

I glanced around, trying to be subtle as I looked for the nomad biker.

Runner raised two fingers to his mouth letting out an ear-splitting whistle. I grimaced but moved closer. From a building on the far right, Wrath emerged, a bag slung over one shoulder, a brown bag in his other hand. I recognised his loose-hipped, confident walk. The way his head moved slightly every now and then, as if he were constantly scoping his surrounds, searching for danger.

My heart gave a weird skip, an ache taking up residence somewhere in my middle.

"We ready?" Runner asked, looking at the assembled group.

"Bikes are loaded, trailer's good," Switch reported.

"Tankers are ready," Jo replied, flicking her braid over her shoulder. "Though not sure your boy's up to the challenge of driving the big rig."

"Baby," Texas drawled, crossing his arms, and giving her a cocky grin. "I know exactly how to handle a big rig."

Runner ignored him, looking to Audrey.

"The comms are loaded and I've plotted the locations where we'll need to offload them. The real issue will be putting them in secure locations."

"We'll deal with that when we get there," Pope said, running a hand through his hair. "The real issue will be hiding the fuel in the safe houses."

"Nope," Wrath commented coming up to the group. He reached across handing me the paper bag and shrugging off the backpack. "The real issue will be keeping out of reach of militia, cults, and bastards."

The pandemic had descended a few years ago, rapidly spreading across the world and forcing border closures and shutting down supply lines. At first, it had looked like we'd overcome it, that it would be a short thing. But then the vaccine had arrived and caused an unexpected result—it'd mutated the disease.

When the world had finally ended, it hadn't been with a bang. Instead, it'd happened with a whimper. Trust had eroded over years as food become scarce and people died. When the government hadn't been able to deliver on basic promises—like a vaccine—society had reverted to violence to survive. When the world finally went dark—the power grid going down, the communications falling silent, it had been an end to a long, painful death.

And yet here we were. Alive. Surviving in the after.

I'd holed up in my University, just me and twelve other women. We'd survived, using our skills to thrive. I was a qualified botanist, and had been completing my doctorate focusing on nanoparticle use to increase crop stress tolerance and yield.

I guess that was now over.

I hadn't planned on ever returning to the Nameless Souls MC. Gus had been a monster, and when I'd finally escaped, I'd made it so he wouldn't find me. Returning had been a nightmare, but I'd done it when The Purge, a rogue cult group that enslaved women, had overrun the College, injuring Ava, and putting us all at risk.

We'd survived that invasion but knew more were on the way. We'd needed help, more protection, so I'd brought them here—to the compound. Throwing myself on my father's mercy had been a deeply shameful humbling experience. But I'd done it, and in return, he'd tried to drug Ellie and sell her into slavery.

He'd been punished for his actions but it didn't stop me from feeling shame. My own blood had tried to harm a woman I deeply respected and loved like a sister.

"Bastards?" Jo asked, drawing my attention back to the group.

Wrath reached out, tapping the brown bag still clutched in my hand. "Eat."

He looked back at Ava. "Bastards, mutated humans."

"Mutated how?" Lottie asked.

He shrugged. "Some are crazy. The virus having corrupted their mind. They're more animal than human but pathetic, easily overpowered. Others are strong, vicious, smart. But their overwhelming desire is to kill or fuck."

"Wait. Wait, wait, wait. Wait a damned second," Audrey said, holding up a hand. "Are you saying there are goddamned zombies out there?"

"No, these beasts aren't dead. They're just corrupted."

A quick glance around the group revealed that only us women were surprised by this news.

"You've seen them?" I asked Wrath. It was my first question to him in over five years. My first words to him since... I pushed the memory away.

He looked at me, his dark eyes staring, questioning, evaluating. Finally, he nodded.

"I've killed them."

A geneticist could explain it better, but our understanding of the disease was that it had mutated from rabies and the common flu. Some kind of highly contagious disease that resulted in fevers, muscle atrophy, breathing difficulties and, eventually, a painful death.

It was only after the virus mutated when the world really went to shit. No one had told us what was happening with the second strain and why the government had tried to keep the knowledge from us. But we'd heard whispers of concentration-like camps set up to exterminate people. Of public and open cleansing of entire families. Of violent outbursts between the infected and the vulnerable.

It didn't surprise me that it had mutated once more, though this time there was no one to suppress the knowledge.

"If I say shoot, you shoot."

The group nodded.

"I'm leading this expedition, but if things go to shit then Runner's up. If Runner falls, it's down to Ghost. If that fails you hole up and when it's safe you get the fuck home." He jerked a thumb at the tankers. "They're gonna attract a fuckload of attention and we have to drive right through cult lands. The odd traveller they don't care about. Our group? It's not something they'll be able to ignore."

I swallowed, nerves twisting in my belly.

He crouched, drawing a quick map in the dirt. "Audrey and Pope, Ava and Ghost will be tail. Jo and Texas, you're gonna drive the tankers. Keep them fast and if shit gets real, you bail. Prospects will flank, Switch on Jo, Zero on Texas. Butcher and Lottie will be in the Wrangler which will lead the tankers in case we need to move shit out of the road. Runner and

Ellie will follow, me and Kate at point." He looked up. "Any questions?"

"I'm riding with you?"

His gaze snapped to me then he looked away. "Yeah. Any other questions?"

Everyone shook their heads.

"Good. Say your goodbyes, we roll out in ten."

He stood dusting off his hands as everyone moved, saying their final goodbyes to friends or family. Doing their last-minute checks for equipment or items. I stood frozen, alone. I'd already said my goodbyes, already triple checked my items.

I felt strangely alone. Bereft. Separated from the people around me.

"Kate."

I looked to Wrath, finding my arms wrapped around myself.

"Eat the fucking food. We've got a long ride and Yana said you didn't have breakfast." He walked off, headed for his bike.

I opened the bag, pulling out a breakfast roll. Egg, bacon, and BBQ sauce on a sesame seed bun. My favourite. Also inside, I found an apple, a wrapped muffin, and a small note.

I pulled the note free, unfolding the crumpled paper.

Kate,

He wanted all your favourite foods. I'm not sure if that means he's interested in you or just a good friend. Either way, I'd jump his bones cause he's hot as fuck.

Love you, stay safe.

Yana.

I unwrapped the roll, taking a large bite as I watched Wrath check over his bike.

He's just a good friend, Yana. No matter how I wish otherwise.

Chapter Three

Wrath

I'd made a huge fucking mistake.

I couldn't say for sure but I was pretty confident I had the biggest hard-on this side of the equator. We were three hours in and had been forced to stop twice to clear a path on the road for the tankers, and yet my fucking cock was harder than a fucking diamond—painful as fuck too.

Kate pressed into my back, her arms locked around my waist as we cruised down the backroads. The day was bright, sunny, but still cool.

Runner cruised up beside me, making a fist. I nodded, slowing as we approached a small dirt truck stop.

Kate waited until we were stopped before jumping off, immediately springing away from me, and busying herself with her helmet.

I couldn't ignore how her scent clung to me, her perfume sticking to my jacket. A floral mix that reminded me of spring and summer, sunshine, and joy.

Things that were sadly lacking in my life.

You wanna go find your balls and stick them back on, you sorry sack of human flesh.

The tankers parked on the road, but the bikes pulled off,

coming to circle.

Audrey pulled her helmet off, shaking out her hair. "This looks alright, but it's gonna be a bitch to find a place to put it."

The one downside to her network was that it needed to be securely located in a high place. Trees were out—too many animals. Anything man-made it would have to be attached to it in a way that made it simultaneously inconspicuous and still able to function.

Fucking nightmare.

"The toilet block?" Pope asked, scoping the dirt lot.

The truck stop contained nothing but a rusty bin, an old picnic table, and a concrete toilet block.

Ava eyed the toilet block. "I could get up that."

"Or you could not," Lottie snapped, coming to our group, and handing Audrey the case containing her transmitter. "Your side is still healing—despite your best efforts."

Ghost moved to the toilet wall. In one swift move, he hauled himself up the side, landing lightly on the roof, barely making a whisper of sound.

"Motherfucker is quiet," Ava muttered.

"You think we call him Ghost for fun?" Pope asked.

Audrey opened the case, propping it on the picnic table to turn it on.

"It'll need to be in a decent sunny position. The solar panels need to be able to recharge. The battery will last longer if we can siphon some of the load off the panels," she told Ghost, lifting the case, and moving to the block.

"Can it get wet?" Pope asked as Ghost leaned down to grab it. He grunted, lifting the heavy case then shimmying back on his belly and moving onto the roof more fully.

Audrey placed a hand on her heart, gasping. "Oh shit, no.

How did I forget to account for weather?" She rolled her eyes. "God save me from idiots. Can it get wet? Of course, it can. Rain, wind, that's all fine as long as it's anchored. It's just the light that's gonna be the real issue."

Kate appeared beside me, holding a cordless drill.

"Ghost, maybe try to drill it down?"

He came back, leaning down to take the offered drill and shifting back up. A moment later we heard it start, the familiar sound of metal shearing metal.

"Good thinking," I told her.

She flushed, ducking her head. "We should have thought of it before we left."

"But we didn't. You did."

Just take the fucking compliment, Kate.

She shrugged, but her face remained flushed.

Ghost jumped down, landing lightly.

"Done?" Ava asked.

He nodded, handing the drill back to Kate.

"Secure?" Audrey asked.

Ghost nodded again, dusting his hands on his jeans.

"Do you even talk?" Ava asked, rolling her eyes.

He looked directly at her, his gaze intense. There was a moment of silence before he answered.

"Only in the bedroom."

And with that, he turned, heading back to his bike.

Audrey flicked open her phone hitting the number two on the pad. We heard it ring then Hazard answered.

"Why the fuck does it say you're number one on my phone? I'm the fucking President," he barked down the line.

"And yet I'm the creator of the Audrey-Network. Suck it up, Prez." She hung up on him with a cackle. "It works, we can go."

Pope laughed, looking around. "Anyone need to pee before we go? No? Just me? Cool. Give me five and we can hit the road."

He headed inside, calling loudly, "Don't listen, Audrey!"

"Ew!" She turned on her heel, falling in beside Kate and me. "That man is gross. I bet he won't wash his hands."

"Pope carries hand sanitizer, soap, and a fucking comb everywhere," I told her. "He's a clean freak."

She blinked. "Huh. Didn't pick that."

I saw Kate smile before she ducked her head again. I gritted my teeth. This shy act didn't sit right with me. The woman I loved—

Shut that the fuck down, brother.

I sucked in a deep breath, once again aware of the press of my cock against the seam of my jeans.

This is gonna be a long fucking ride to Queensland.

Chapter Four

Kate

There were two ways to drive to Queensland. The first had been via the coastal highway. It passed through major towns and cities, beautiful but quick.

In the before, it would have been the preference. In the after, that was asking for trouble.

Instead, we chose the back way. The highway would take us through backcountry, travelling through bush and tiny country towns. They may or may not be abandoned depending on the locals, but they were more manageable than the desperados starving in the cities. From everything I'd heard about this trip in the lead-up, country people fell into one of two piles. Live and let live, or shoot first, ask later.

We passed through two blink-and-you'll-miss-it towns, both no more than a grocery store, a pub, and a post office—all long since raided and abandoned. Wrath had stopped us at the next town, showing us to the back of the post office.

"This is a stop for nomads," he explained unlocking the combination on the padlocked post box. He swung the door open, revealing two packages. The first contained food which he swapped out with our freeze-dried stores. The next contained three notepads, a red, a blue, and a yellow, as well as a pencil and a pen.

Wrath flicked through the blue notebook, finding a page that had been dog-eared and ripped it out. He tucked the paper in his pocket, then added a note explaining the food and that the compound was safe.

"It's in code. Nomads know the code," he explained, dog-earing the page, and replacing the books. "Every stop has the same three notepads. The blue ones are what we use at the moment. The other two are spares. God knows what we'll do once we run out of paper." He shot Audrey a look. "Better hope your communications work."

"Bitch, please. It's gonna work."

Wrath shut the box, locking it. He scooped up a handful of dirt, throwing it over the box.

He caught my questioning look. "Gotta make it look abandoned."

Smart.

We'd then driven for the next few hours, occasionally stopping to offload Audrey's transmitters, stealing toilet breaks, or snacking in those stolen moments of pause. The whole day we'd only seen one other human being, a man with a shotgun leading two cows. He'd watched us from a tended field, his eyes narrowed, his gun raised as we passed.

It was now late, the sun having long since set. My face felt numb, my hands frozen as Wrath guided us down a series of backroads, until they turned to gravel and eventually dirt.

Wrath slowed, the bike bumping down the road until we came to a small hut beside a giant river.

He stopped the bike, killing the engine then helped me off.

"You good?" he asked, reaching out to steady me.

I nodded. "J-j-just cold." My legs also felt like jelly and my body still buzzed from the vibrations of the bike. It'd been a while since I'd ridden so far. Not since—

I stopped that line of thinking, cutting off the memory before it could take form.

"Go sit in the truck, I'll be a little while."

He let me go, stepping back and I immediately wished for his warmth. I wrapped my arms around myself, watching him walk to the small hut, gun out, opening the door with extreme caution.

Ava came up beside me, Ghost beside her. "What's he doing?"

"I'm not sure," I answered, shivering. "He said he'd be a while."

Ava watched him, a hand on the gun at her waist. "Go sit in the car, Kate."

I sighed, annoyed that once again I was relegated to the child's table. "Fine."

I walked to the parked Wrangler and hopped in the back, shoving over a few bags to make room. Lottie twisted in her seat, brushing hair back from her small face. "What's happening?"

"No idea." I grabbed a blanket from the floor, tugging it up and over me. "Hopefully we're stopping."

"It's a pit stop," Butcher confirmed. "But we'll be waiting a while. Wrath has to muster the troops."

"What?"

Butcher grinned, sending a look my way. "You'll see."

I settled, chatting quietly with Lottie, sharing a protein bar then snuggling into the door when she decided to get out and go chat with Audrey, Ellie, and Ava.

I woke to a bump.

"Ouch!" I snapped a hand to my head rubbing the spot that had cracked on the window. "What's happening?"

"Sorry!" Butcher called. "But we're next."

I shifted, looking out the front windscreen and blinking at the sight.

"It's a barge."

He followed Wrath and Runner onto the boat, parking it at the front. I twisted in my seat, seeing the two tankers begin to load onto the ship.

"Where are we going?"

"Middle of the river. It's the safest place for us tonight."

The barge bobbed as Jo drove the tanker, pulling it to a stop just a whisper behind the Wrangler. She sent me a wave, putting it into park and shutting off the engine. Texas followed quickly, with the remaining bikes falling in behind. I got out, wrapping the blanket around my shoulders, and coming to stand beside Jo as we watched a small crew shuffle around the deck, getting ready to raise the ramp and set off.

"Have to admit, I wasn't expecting this," she said, moving to lean into me. I offered her an edge of the blanket and she accepted, wrapping it around her shoulders and snuggling into me. "A shitty tent, yeah. Maybe even a farmhouse if we were lucky. A barge? Hell no."

"Complaining, Jo-Jo?" Texas asked, coming up behind us. She stiffened beside me, shooting him a death glare.

"Was I speaking to you?"

He grinned, leaning against the truck, his stance casual. "If you're cold you could come snuggle with me." He sent a wink my way. "I wouldn't kick either of you out."

"I'd rather eat shit," Jo retorted turning her back on him.

Texas had joined the chapter in the years since I'd been gone. But it hadn't taken me long to realise he was sweet on Jo, and she was determined to hate his guts.

I watched as Wrath moved about the deck, chatting with the crew, and checking in with the prospects and Runner. He slowly made his way to our little group, his gaze on me.

"We can go below deck. The cabins are made up and our chef will have dinner ready shortly."

"We're safe here?" Jo asked, flicking a hand out towards the crew. "Just saying, they look shifty as fuck."

"They're good people. I've already bartered our night. And they know better than to fuck over the Nameless Souls."

"What was the price?" I asked, my stomach clenching.

Wrath considered me. "Fuel and fresh food. We brought extra for bartering so it's not an issue. We'll be safe tonight."

"That's it? But there are no women." The words flew from my mouth before I could stop them.

Wrath frowned. "The women are below deck. They protect their families, Kate. Just like we protect ours."

I nodded, suddenly ashamed. "Of course, sorry."

He reached out, tucking a stray hair behind my ear. "We don't barter family, babe. We're not your father."

I blinked, tears stinging my eyes. "I know."

He looked at me, his dark eyes intense.

"Yo, lovebirds," Pope called from the front of the barge, breaking the tension between us.

Wrath broke our stare, twisting to look over his shoulder at Pope.

"We eating or what?"

Or what indeed.

Chapter Five

Kate

The belly of the barge had been extensively renovated. It had morphed from a large storage area into a series of rooms each sectioned off for families.

"We'll have to bed down in the common room," Wrath explained, reaching out to steady me as I climbed down the narrow, steep stairs. "But it's warm and comfortable."

The common room was a large sitting area, filled with faded cushions and bean bags, low coffee tables set here and there in amongst the bunches of seating.

"Welcome!" a man greeted with a smile, opening his arms. "Come in, dinner won't be long. Make yourselves at home."

"This is Brock," Wrath said, nodding in the man's direction. "Captain and leader of the Spirit."

"And an all-round awesome guy to know," Brock said with a bow. "My home is yours for tonight."

We took seats across the area, the crew slowly trickling in and joining us. Kids appeared, looking shy but interested. Women joined the area and I couldn't help but notice how well they looked and how freely they moved around.

Safe.

Platters of food were brought out, items meant to be eaten

with fingers. Pita bread, fresh and doughy; lettuce cups with fragrant rice and beans stuffed inside; delicious morsels of capsicum and ground meat perfumed with herbs and luscious salt.

"This is delicious," Jo declared around a mouthful. "Fucking compliments to the chef."

"My wife will be happy to hear your approval." Brock smiled, lifting a bottle in her direction. He lazed on pillows, looking for all the world like a modern pirate, or perhaps a Han Solo wanna be.

"Did you run this ship in the before?" Lottie asked, scooping up the remains on her plate with a slice of pita.

"We did. Some of the guys have come to us since, but most were part of my crew long before."

"It's a good idea," Ava noted patting the ground beside her. "Keep moving, keep shifting, safety in mobility."

"But we're getting low on fuel," Brock admitted. "We're having to send our scavengers further and further afield. And our last crew have yet to return."

Ellie tipped her head. "Diesel?"

My stomach clenched as Runner placed a hand on her leg, cautioning her.

Good.

"Yes."

Ellie nodded, glancing up at Runner, seeking permission.

Bitter anxiety burned the back of my throat.

I need to get out of here.

I pushed up, excusing myself quietly as Runner began to question Brock about what options they were exploring.

I didn't want to be there, didn't want the anxiety that came along with listening to people talk in circles, playing games until they finally reached an understanding.

I'd learned early that nothing came for free, not even the air we breathed.

I moved around the room, taking in the murals painted on walls. Dreamtime paintings decorated the roughshod walls, images of stories of the creation of this land.

"Are you familiar with the story of Weowi, the water spirit?" an old woman asked, coming up beside me.

I shook my head. "I'm not. But it's beautiful. The art is gorgeous."

"My daughter's work," the woman said, pressing a hand to her heart. "She's deeply connected to our land and our stories." She looked at me, her gaze considering. "You're the botanist."

I nodded.

"Do the plants call to you, sister?"

I tilted my head, considering her words. "Perhaps. I always feel better when I'm surrounded by plants and there's dirt under my nails."

She reached out, capturing one of my hands and lifting it to examine my fingers. She grinned, then dropped my hand, gesturing. "Come with me." She led me out of the dining area and down a short hall to a door at the rear of the barge. It had on it a label in child's handwriting, *plant room,* a tree painted beside it.

The woman pushed the door open and I sucked in a breath, warm heat flowed out to me, the scent of rich earth, wet ground, and fresh air mingled with the unique fragrance of organic life.

"Our greenhouse," the woman said, inviting me in.

I stepped through the door, my hands immediately reaching out to brush the branches of the lemon tree closest to me.

The room was set up like a hydroponic studio. Rows and rows of plants each type within a shelf set-up, able to be rotated to receive the right amount of artificial light, air, and water.

"This is amazing," I whispered, finding myself in awe of their efforts. Lettuce and cabbage, carrots and peas, citrus, sweet potato, sunflowers. Each product had been lovingly curated and gently grown to ensure it was robust and healthy.

"Come," the woman said, gesturing me down an aisle, "down here is the plant I need help with."

She led me to a small work area. A long wooden bench, tools neatly positioned above it. Below, there were shelves filled with boxes with different labelled goods, things like seaweed solution. On the bench sat a large bonsai, its roots gnarled, it's trunk aged.

"Hello," I greeted, placing my hands on its pot. "Aren't you beautiful."

"She is my great-great-grandmother's," the woman told me. "A gift given in exchange for hospitality."

I turned her pot then frowned, leaning closer. Her trunk had a crack, small but painful.

"She was damaged when we had to flee. And while I can tend to most of her needs, this is beyond my expertise."

I nodded, examining the damage. "Do you have some wire, pliers, and a sharp knife?"

The woman shuffled about pulling out the things I needed and placing them on the bench. I picked up the knife and gently scraped it against the separated wood.

"In future, if this happens again, you'll want to fuse the broken parts quickly. But because there's been some healing, but very poorly, I'm removing the diseased area and opening it to new healing." I blew gently, removing the scrapings and checked the cut. "Now." I placed the knife down and picked up the wire, twisting a loop in one end and wrapping the wire around the trunk. "You need to fuse them together." I pointed at the tiny gap. "Twist this looped end and it'll force them closer. When they stay that way for long enough, they'll grow back together." I twisted the loop, tightening the wire until the break closed.

"There," I said with a grin, setting down the pliers. "She'll always have the scar, but with time she'll recover."

The woman took my hand, placing it on the bonsai's base, my palm over the gnarled roots. "She thanks you."

My heart felt full as I caressed the beautiful tree. "And I thank her and you for letting me help."

"You should stay here. We could use your skills." The woman placed a hand on her chest. "And you may call me Auntie or Rita."

An honour.

I grinned, dipping my head. "Thank you, Auntie. I'm Kate." I looked back at the bonsai. "And as much as I would love to stay and help with your garden, my brother is back home, and we have friends and family to help before I can return to him."

"No, you don't," Wrath's voice broke the moment, and had me jumping in fright.

"W-w-wrath! Geez, you s-s-scared me."

Auntie didn't appear to be surprised by his presence.

"Your brothers aren't back at the compound," he repeated, frowning at me. "One's at the Plantation, the others I have no fucking clue."

I blinked. "Ice didn't tell y-y-you?"

Wrath's mouth twisted. "Tell me what?"

I hesitated, a core part of me knowing this would change us, and rebelling against the uncertainty.

"Speak truth," Auntie Rita admonished.

"Ice is my b-b-brother. Half-brother," I corrected. "Gus is our f-f-father."

Wrath froze, his body cut from stone.

"I assumed he'd told you. Everyone f-f-found out when he needed surgery."

"No. He didn't." Wrath's voice was low, gruff, his body still motionless, as if anchored down.

Silence won for a moment.

"Right, you two obviously have unresolved issues." Auntie Rita clapped me on the shoulder. "If you change your mind, we'd welcome you."

She moved, leaving the workspace, her humming growing fainter as she moved through the room. The sound of a door opening and shutting behind her left Wrath and I in silence, the only sound the low drone of the engines below us, and the hum of the lights that helped the plants to grow.

The way Wrath looked at me was... confusing. He didn't give me an insight into his thoughts. Not a twitch of his lips, not a frown, nothing. He was a blank slate.

"S-s-say something," I finally said, desperate to break this unbearable silence between us.

"You're not in love with Ice."

I shook my head, then nodded, then shook it again. "Yes, I mean, I-I-I am in that I l-l-love him like a brother. He's my favourite person in the world. But no, not romantically. I mean, I'm not a Lannister."

Wrath's mouth didn't even twitch at the *Game of Thrones'* reference.

Shit.

"Why didn't you tell me?"

I sighed, reaching up to tuck a stray hair behind my ear. "Because he asked me n-n-not to. And he was the only family I had l-l-left who was worth a damn. I didn't want to lose him."

Wrath's eyebrows twitched, the tiniest of frowns marring his brow. "Did he know?"

"Know?"

"Where you were. This whole time, did he know?"

I hesitated, then nodded. "He was the only one. Well, he and G-G-Ghost. Gus sent Ghost to find me, which he did. Easily. But I-I-Ice intervened."

Wrath absorbed this information, his face still blank. "Did you think about me?"

Air stuck in my chest, my breath catching. "W-what?"

His mask still in place, Wrath took a step closer, then another, backing me up until my back hit the workbench, preventing me from moving further. He crowded in, leaning over me, his face close to mine. Only when he was this close could I see, he wasn't impassive—no. He was enraged. His eyes lit with an unholy light.

"Did. You. Think. About. Me," he repeated, slowly, his teeth gritted, his arms by his side, fists clenching and unclenching, as if he were trying to control himself.

"I… I don't—"

"Yes or no, Kate."

"Y-yes," I whispered, the response automatic. "A-a-all the time."

"When."

I hesitated but his hand came up, cupping my jaw, forcing me to look into his searching eyes. That touch was a truth serum, the warmth of his hand loosening my tongue. I was powerless to stop the words from flowing.

"After you left. B-b-before you left. When we were t-t-together. When we were apart. When I was s-s-studying, or planting or w-w-walking, or a million other times." I admitted, tears stinging my eyes.

"In bed?"

I couldn't deny it, didn't even try. He'd see through any lie I tried to tell.

"Yes."

Chapter Six

Wrath

"Yes."

My mind reeled, my body aching as I processed Kate's whispered admission. All these godforsaken years she'd been mine.

Fuck.

My control snapped, my heart setting my body in motion before my mind could catch up.

Mine. Mine. Mine.

My lips descended, hovering for a moment, a tenuous breath before tasting the lips which I'd fantasized about for years.

Under me, Kate gasped, her hands coming up to clutch my vest.

Was she going to push me away? Pull me closer?

She didn't move, just clutched the fabric as I devoured her with hungry passion. I caught her bottom lip between mine, sucking and nipping, her mouth falling open, allowing me to take advantage and surge forward, my tongue sliding across hers.

My hips pressed into her and for one moment I thought she would shove me aside. Instead, she pressed back. A mewing sound escaping her.

I bent, cupping her glorious arse, lifting her onto the workbench, encouraging her to wrap her thick thighs around my waist as I pressed my cock to her core.

"Wrath," she gasped, her head falling back. Her hands fisted in my hair, her greedy body clenching around me. "Please."

"Please what?" I panted, my hands running up her sides. "Please let me touch your breasts? Let me lick your nipples? Please let me fuck your tight little snatch?"

She shuddered, her eyes opening, desire and want warring for dominance. "Yes."

"Which one?"

"All of it."

I grinned, knowing it was pure sin, knowing she liked that look on my face. "You're gonna regret giving me that permission, Sunshine."

My hands went to the hem of her shirt, pulling until it slid up her body, revealing soft skin and glorious curves.

Her breasts, encased in a no-nonsense black bra, were perfection.

I dropped her top, my hands immediately moving to cup her over the fabric. "Fuck," I muttered, leaning forward, needing to taste her mouth again. "You're fucking perfect."

She tilted her head, giving me access to her mouth. We kissed as I stroked thumbs over her nipples, knowing the fabric would lessen the impact.

But she reacted like a lightning rod at my touch. Her breath catching, her fingers clenching, her thighs tightening every time my thumbs moved.

She was electric, wanton, full of untamed wild.

My cock ached, throbbing and bucking, I fucking knew I wouldn't last long once I got inside her.

I removed her bra, my mouth replacing my fingers, her whispered pants of encouragement flaming us to burn brighter.

My tongue swirled, glorying in the taste of her skin, licking and sucking, marking her, tattooing this memory into my soul.

Mine. Mine. Mine.

Dimly, I heard the door open, voices coming from the entry.

"As you can see—"

"Get out," I yelled, only barely pausing. "Get the fuck out!"

Against me, Kate stiffened, her body going rigid.

"And like I was saying, I'll show you this room later," I heard Brock correct, laughter in his voice. I couldn't see him through the vines and shelves, but I heard the door shut, sealing Kate and me in once more.

I looked down, my body desperate for hers. She blinked up at me, her cheeks and chest flushed a delicious pink.

"This was…." She trailed off, her hands dropping to my shoulders. "Unexpected."

I huffed out a laugh. "Was it though? We've been circling each other for years. Only a matter of time before one of us broke."

She tipped her head to the side, a small grin playing at her lips. "I'll note it was you first."

"And thank Christ I'm the smart one," I replied, moving in to start kissing her again. A hand to my chest halted my movement.

"Wrath, I…." She bit her lower lip. "I need to tell you; this is pretty unfamiliar territory for me."

"What, making out on a barge? First time for everything, Sunshine."

"No, I mean… all of this." She gestured between us. "I'm kind of, umm… inexperienced."

I blinked, slowly. Processing this news took me a minute. "What do you mean inexperienced?"

She sucked in a breath. "Like, that may have been my first kiss?"

I blinked again. Distantly aware of how fucking stupid I must look but unable to process the knowledge that this girl wasn't just mine. She was *mine.*

"I mean, I'm not totally inexperienced. I mean, I touch myself and I watched porn in the before. And I read a lot of romance. Like really dirty romance. But I've just never—"

I cut her off with a hard kiss. Hard, dirty, and so fucking possessive. I poured all of my feelings into that kiss, fucking her mouth with my tongue, branding her lips with mine. Every dirty, filthy, possessive feeling I'd ever had about this woman was in that fucking kiss.

"Kate," I told her, finally breaking the kiss but keeping my forehead pressed to hers. "Tonight, all we're gonna do is get you off. When we get to the ranch, I'm gonna strip you naked and fuck you raw. I won't be able to help myself. You understand? Even right now is testing me."

She nodded, her breathing choppy. "I understand."

"Good." I dropped my hands, one hand going to her zipper, the other to her back. "Lean back, Sunshine."

She tilted, giving me access to her jeans. I unzipped them, sliding the fly apart and slipping my hand inside.

Soaked. Fucking saturated.

"Fucking fuck fuck," I barked closing my eyes and sucking in a deep breath. I opened my eyes, pegging her with a glare. "You're trying my fucking patience, Kate. This." I pressed a finger against her wet underwear. She sucked in a breath, her body jerking in response. "This is making it really fucking hard for me to wait for a goddamned private room with a bed."

"I don't mind," Kate replied, her voice shaky. "I don't mind if we do it here."

"But I do."

I pulled aside her underwear with a finger, slipping through her wetness. I zeroed in on her clit, knowing we were both too on edge tonight to fuck around.

I whispered a brief apology then let go, working her tight little cunt. I swirled and circled, pressed and teased, finding what made Kate gasp and moan, what made her whimper and beg. She liked her right side more than her left. She liked slow and gentle to start, then hard and fast as she got closer. She hated swirls but loved circles. She didn't like when I was silent and shattered when I talked dirty, praising her, calling her my good girl.

"You gonna come, Sunshine?" I asked, pressing and circling, revving her up, knowing I'd likely come just from the beauty of watching her.

She nodded, her eyes glazed, her cheeks flushed, sweat dotted her brow, her lips swollen from my kisses.

"Good girl," I praised, pressing in, circling faster. Under me, her cunt clenched, her legs jerking, wet coated my fingers, my palm, as her body broke, her orgasm washing over me.

Kate didn't come with a scream, but a satisfied sigh, my name on her lips.

"Wrath."

And fuck if that didn't make me feel like a fucking champion.

She fell into me, her arms circling my body.

I wanted to taste her, to lick her off my fingers and then start over, this time with my mouth on her pussy, my tongue tasting every drop.

But I didn't. Despite the desire riding my arse, and the overwhelming need to claim her, to flip her over and fuck her on this rickety workbench, I remained still, patting and soothing her, letting her find comfort after the heaviness of that release.

Finally, she pulled back, making a face. "I smell like sex."

I grinned. "You smell fucking amazing."

She rolled her eyes. "Is there a shower on this boat."

"Sure."

She waited then laughed, pushing at my chest playfully. "Wrath!"

"Oh, you want me to tell you where it is?" I pulled her into my chest again, lifting her then setting her on the floor but not letting her go. "I'll tell you, if you promise me one thing."

"What?" she asked, narrowing her eyes on me.

"You'll let me watch."

Her eyebrows lifted and she blushed a bright red. "No, try again."

I rolled my eyes. "Fine, just sleep with me tonight. Just sleep. I want to be close to you."

Despite the boner.

She hesitated, dropping her gaze for a moment, then nodded. "I'd like that."

I dropped my hands to her fly, doing her up, taking care of my woman. That done, I slung an arm around her shoulders, pulling her into me.

"Then let's see about that shower, Sunshine."

Chapter Seven

Kate

I woke to something poking my back and a heavy weight over my hips. I felt warm and protected.

It took me a moment to realise the warmth at my back was a human, the weight was an arm, and the thing poking me had to be an erection.

I shifted, rolling, and then blinked down at Wrath who watched me with sleepy eyes. "Get back here," he told me gruffly, his voice rough with sleep. "It's still early."

I hesitated for a moment then gave in, the warmth of him and the comfort I found in his arms far outweighed any anxiety or embarrassment I might have felt.

I snuggled back under the blanket, Wrath's arms immediately locking around me, pulling me into him, this time my front to his.

"I see some parts of you are awake," I murmured as his erection pressed into my belly.

"Ignore him," Wrath mumbled, settling his head on mine, and gently stroking my back. "He's a dick."

I chuckled softly, then fell into silence, drifting as the barge engines hummed under our bodies, and the sleeping people around us slowly began to stir. I must have dozed off, because the next time I woke people had begun to dress around me, packing up their sleeping bags and blankets, while the smell of cooking hung in the air.

"I have to get up, don't I?" I asked the big mass of solid muscle before me.

"Mm, probably," Wrath answered, his hand sliding down under the blanket to cup my arse. Just that touch felt amazing. "Looking forward to a week in bed with you though."

I flushed, pleasure and anticipation igniting my senses. Wrath slowly unwrapped from around me, moving to a stand then helping me up. Together, we rolled up the bedding. He handed me my jeans. We'd slept in our clothes, ready for a quick escape if needed. The only concession to comfort was a pair of leggings I wore instead of the rough material.

I went to the bathroom, taking the time to clean up and swap over my clothing. Toothpaste was a commodity, but luckily for us, the compound had inherited a massive store of tooth powder—just add water.

Clean and relatively presentable I returned to the barge's common area, finding breakfast laid out for us. A generous if simple meal. The spread consisted of freshly churned butter, still warm bread, jams, and fresh scrambled eggs. I helped myself, scooping a thick layer of jam onto the fluffy bread, moaning at the delicious taste.

Brock sat with our party again, scratching his chin. "We'll be at the next drop off point shortly. Be warned, I know you're on your way to Queensland and we've heard rumours of towns between here and the border who have had a rough winter. There are whispers of slavers patrolling the areas and cannibals.

Not to mention the bastards roaming about the place."

Bastards, the mutated humans Wrath had mentioned.

"Have you seen a bastard?" Audrey asked, reaching for the coffee pot.

Brock pushed up from his reclined position on the pillows, lifting his shirt. A wide bandage wrapped around his ribs. "We had a run-in about two weeks ago. Found a little tug boat drifting down the river. The crew must have been turned at some point. Highly emaciated yet still deadly. Managed to get a good punch in, broke three ribs before we finally killed the monsters."

I grimaced, the bread no longer sitting so well in my stomach.

"They're moving south," Wrath muttered, shaking his head. He looked to Ghost. "Last I'd heard they were mostly contained in the northern states. If they're moving south that's not a great sign."

Ghost nodded, his expression grim.

"What did your letter say?" Runner asked.

Wrath pulled it out of his pocket unfolding the paper and examining it. I peeked over his shoulder, the symbols, swirls, and numbers making no logical sense.

"It's from Rain, another nomad. His last contact was with the Cunnamulla Chapter. He says that the fuel lines are low along this stretch. He tried the coast but ran into a group of cultists seeking women. Says they had a stockpile of weapons they'd managed to barter from a militia group. Looks like most are starting to settle in various areas rather than move about. But that's causing issues as food becomes scarce. He was headed to the compound but looking to stop in and check on a friend before then." Wrath folded the paper, tucking it back into his pocket. "The rest is just gossip."

I tried not to think about how lonely an existence it must be for these nomads. They had no home chapter but had become the lifeline between us. Without communications, they had become our only option for news.

But they moved alone, relying on themselves to survive.

I shivered, immensely grateful that Wrath was now here with me.

Runner pushed to his feet, dusting his front. "We should get moving. We don't want to expose your people for longer than necessary when we make land."

Brock stood, holding out a hand. "Appreciate that, brother."

Jo stumbled in a moment later, bleary-eyed, and filthy. She yawned widely as she dropped to the floor, reaching for a slice of bread.

"It's done," she said, looking at Brock. "You'll need to test her out, but your mechanic can iron out the kinks. Main thing is she's ready."

"Did I miss something?" I asked.

Jo stifled another yawn, bringing the bread to her mouth and taking a large bite. She groaned, closing her eyes, and chewing for a moment before answering.

"This barge was a steamer, back in another life. She still had all the parts sitting there but had been converted to diesel back in the mid-1900s. Me and their mechanic spent the night checking her over and making the necessary changes to convert her back." Jo shrugged. "Means they can use other fuel sources when the diesel gets scarce."

"Our thanks," Brock said with a grin. "If it works then you can ride on the Spirit for free anytime you require."

Jo waved her hand dismissively. "Don't get your hopes up. She hasn't been used as a steamer for decades. There might be something we missed. And God knows you're not gonna be able to go as fast on steam power. Not to mention the additional weight from having to carry a fuel load."

Brock shrugged. "Time is all relative and speed means nothing if we're dead on the water. To be still is to die, to move is to live."

Jo shrugged, tearing off another chunk. "Your life, dude."

Texas watched her with a frown. "And who's gonna drive the rig with you so fucking tired?"

Butcher raised a hand. "She already checked it over with me."

"And I'll drive the SUV," Lottie said. "It's no big deal."

Ava sighed, pushing to her feet. "It's a good thing I have confidence in your driving abilities otherwise I'd be fucking worried right now."

Lottie laughed, moving to wrap her sister in a hug. "You're the one who taught me the defensive techniques. Don't worry, I've got this."

Wrath and I followed them out. I shivered as we stepped into the early morning wind, the sun still low in the sky.

"We got thirty minutes before we hit the port," Wrath yelled over the wind. I turned the collar of my jacket up, hunkering down, trying to protect myself from the wind.

"Let's check the bikes."

The barge pulled around, beginning to move into place as we did our preparations. Tanks were refuelled, wheels and gears checked. Jo appeared, clean but with damp hair and dark circles under her eyes. She climbed into the SUV, settling into the front passenger seat, and immediately fell asleep.

Wrath handed me my helmet, then gestured at the land. "When we hit that we're leaving straight away. The less time we're here the better."

I nodded, looking around for Auntie Rita. I found her on the upper deck, watching from a protected alcove. I lifted my hand, giving her a wave. She did the same, inclining her head just a little before disappearing from view.

Wrath settled on his bike and I joined him, squeezing myself nice and close. He started her up, the bike vibrating under us as the barge ramp slowly lowered. He reached down, patting my knee just before the ramp hit the ground. Once down and settled, a crew member nodded at Wrath and he took off, easily rolling down and onto the dirt track on the other side. Runner and Ellie followed, then Lottie and Jo in the SUV, the two tankers driven by Butcher and Texas, then Zero and Switch.

Once everyone was off, we took off, picking up speed and bumping over the dirt road at a jarring pace.

I tried not to grimace. We hit bitumen after a half-hour and within ten minutes were pulling off into a small farmhouse that sat abandoned by the roadside.

Runner, Ava, and Wrath cleared it while Ghost and Zero kept lookout. Audrey jumped off Pope's bike, quickly scrambling onto the roof to set up her transmitter. Wrath signalled to Butcher to back the tanker up to the house.

"What's happening?" I asked Ava when she emerged from the house.

"They're offloading fuel in the basement. There's a tank down there and it's all protected from scavengers." She looked impressed. "Wouldn't have even realised there was a basement if they hadn't shown me the secret door."

I wanted to see, but also knew we were being quick to avoid detection. Danger was an ever-present theme of our daily lives.

Ava leaned in, keeping her voice low. "You okay?" She tipped her head towards Wrath. "The guy's pretty intense. Don't wanna see you hurt."

I offered her a grin, appreciating her concern. Ava was a hard nut to crack. She'd come to us care of Lottie, who'd been studying at the College. She'd walked in, overflowing with weapons and a pissed-off attitude. She'd been on medical leave when the world went to shit. When the virus began mutating and women became a disproportionate statistic, the defence force had dismissed all its women, ordering them into quarantine. She'd made it to us in the dying stages of the before. She'd never said what she'd had to do to make it, but I'd known it hadn't been pretty. She'd been world-weary and angry for a long time.

But she was also the reason we'd survived so long by ourselves. Ava didn't shy away from hard. She looked danger in the eye and pulled the trigger. When scavengers and scouts for The Purge had arrived, we'd dispatched them easily. She'd taken care of us, teaching us survival skills and how to handle weapons. Showing us easy low-tech security options, and creating a sense of community and safety where before there had been little.

I knew this adjustment was hard for her. MCs were inherently male-centric. These men were all alpha all the time. They could be misogynistic, taking over and fuck the consequences. She wasn't used to being seen as a soft female, nor did it suit her. Ava was brains and brawn, guts and glory, feminine and fierce all at once. And she protected those she loved.

And I loved that she had accepted me into her small family.

"I'm good," I told her, reaching out and placing a hand on

her arm. "Really good."

"You knew him?"

I nodded. "In the before. When I lived with Gus after my mum died. It was a nightmare but Wrath and Ice made it bearable."

She gave me a quick look before gazing back out at the fields, her eyes narrowed, constantly searching for dangers. "You hung up on him?"

I laughed. "Oh yeah."

"He good in bed?"

I thought of last night and blushed. Wrath had played my body beautifully, his fingers finding the exact points that made my nerve endings sing until I'd lost myself in a crescendo of feeling.

"Oh yes."

She grinned, her eyes still on the fields. "Good. Don't settle for less than stellar sex… and a man who listens."

My eyebrows raised in surprise at that last comment. I opened my mouth to ask her a question but she snapped upright, her arms swinging her rifle up.

"Get the girls and get inside, we got company."

Chapter Eight

Kate

I moved quickly, signalling the women to follow me. They did, coming inside the house. Outside, the tanker switched off, likely Pope reducing the noise.

Wrath went on alert as we all settled, crouching down below the windows. He moved to me, his lips pressing to my ear.

"Report."

I twisted my head, my lips coming to his ear. "Ava spotted something in the field."

Wrath pulled his pistols free from the holsters at his hip and back. He nodded at Runner giving him a meaningful look. Runner nodded back, crouching, and moving to the door.

Looked like Runner was our bodyguard.

I pulled the weapon in my own holster free, holding it as Ava had taught me, the safety still on.

Point and shoot at the biggest part. Once you hit, go for the chest or head. One hit may slow them, two should stop them, three for the kill. If you miss, try again. If you go down, aim for the parts that hurt.

I silently repeated Ava's training in my head. Her instructions had been drilled into each of us over and over, the months slipping into a jumbled blur.

Outside there was movement. The women beside me all pulled out their own weapons, expressions grim. Above us, I heard Audrey scramble on the roof, her movements creaking against the metal roofing.

"I've got a visual! It's a group of bastards!" I heard Switch roar a moment before guns began to fire.

Runner stood, coming to the window, looking out, his gun braced, his expression grim. "Fuck, it's a horde."

I didn't know what a horde meant, but it damn sure didn't sound good.

Runner swore. "We gotta go." He moved, pointing at Ellie and Lottie. "Close the tank, then push the pipe out the window." He looked at me and Jo. "Guns out, stand at the ready. When we move, we gotta move fast."

We nodded, standing at the ready. Lottie and Ellie made quick work of the tank and pipe, removing, and closing it up and re-securing the trapdoor. They looped the pipe, rolling it up to the window and pushing it outside with a loud thump.

Runner immediately pushed them both back, shoving them behind him.

A face appeared in the window, tattered and scarred, filthy with dirt, grime, and old blood. Perhaps it had once been a human, a man no older than thirty. But now it was a shell of a human, all compassion and emotion gone from his cloudy eyes. In its place was nothing but a beast. Nothing but violence on its mind. He gnashed his teeth at the window, drawing back an arm to punch through the glass, likely trying to rip the frame free to get to us.

Runner blew his head off, glass and blood spraying across

the ground.

"Let's go," he ordered, opening the door and emerging. Jo followed, Ellie and Lottie in the middle, now in possession of their own guns. I trailed, bringing up the rear, responsible for protecting our backs.

My heart hammered in my chest, as time seemed to both speed up and slow down. Everything felt as if it took no more than a fraction of a moment, and yet I couldn't seem to make myself move faster. I felt as if I were in molasses, struggling to move through the sticky, suffocating substance.

Bastards were everywhere, at least twenty of them in the front yard, more still coming, seemingly surging from all directions in their mindless pursuit of blood and violence.

Runner felled two, leading us to the SUV. Ava battled one, hand-to-hand, Ghost at her side taking on three who had swarmed. I lifted my gun, firing at a fourth who appeared from the field, running for them. She went down, collapsing and twitching but staying down.

One jumped off the roof, flying towards me. I lifted my gun, squeezing the trigger. It hit him in the chest, but he collapsed on top of me, his body pinning me to the ground, knocking the air from my lungs and the gun from my hand.

He gnashed his teeth, once, twice, his blood soaking my clothing, as I jerked my hand up and under his neck, pushing his face away, desperate to keep him from biting me. I fell back as he was jerked off me, my back crashing into the dirt under me. Fisting the bastard's hair, Wrath lifted the monster's head, pressing a gun to his temple. A bullet mutilated the side of his head before Wrath tossed the body aside as if it were garbage. He reached down, pulling me to a stand, kicking my gun to me.

"Hurry," he ordered. "On the bike, now." We moved, both of us shooting and kicking, Wrath shoving, as we moved to the bike. The SUV roared to life, Lottie behind the wheel, her face pale but determined as she revved it, directing the fortified vehicle at a new line of emerging bastards, ploughing into them with horrifying efficiency.

We made it to Wrath's bike, and I slid on, quickly getting it running while he provided cover. He killed a final bastard then jumped on, one hand wrapping around my waist, the other holding a pistol to continue shooting.

"Go!"

I went, nearly losing control as a bastard fell in front of us, the bike kicking and bucking as I rode over it, his body making awful sounds as I crunched and squished across infected skin.

The tankers peeled out, their wheels crunching over bastards too slow to move.

"Where's Ava?" I screamed over my shoulder, the wind snatching my words.

Wrath twisted looking around. From the deepest pack, the SUV emerged, mowing a path through the bastards, bodies flying as if this were an action film and not real life.

Behind, shooting and ducking low over their bikes flew Ava and Ghost, their bodies covered in blood, their faces grim as they continued to shoot, kicking out at any bastard that got too close.

I looked around, the women were in the SUV, Runner and Ellie on his bike. Audrey was hanging from the top of the tanker, her face pale as she death gripped the side. Pope rode alongside, his head constantly tilting up to check Audrey's grip.

Switch gripped the back of one of the tankers, attempting to snatch the fuel pipe that bucked and swung on the ground behind.

I moved up, joining in the main pack, looking around to count our numbers.

Zero.

He rode his bike, crouched over, face pale, one hand clutched to his chest.

With the road clear ahead of us, I chanced a look behind. Bastards followed but they were getting smaller, their numbers significantly reduced and their speed much slower than the initial wave.

We rode until we could no longer see them. Then continued riding until Zero's bike began to weave on the road, his body slumping, his skin now a terrible grey.

Wrath signalled me to pull over on the shoulder of the road ahead and I cruised, keeping our machines running. Zero slid off the bike, falling to the ground, his arm clutched to his chest. Lottie and Butcher jumped out, immediately moving to him.

Zero's hand was a mess. One of the bastards had bitten him, ripping a finger clean off and polluting the wound. The blood was dark and murky, filthy with whatever their blood had morphed into.

"Is he turning?" Audrey asked, her hair wild. She'd managed to climb down from the top of the tanker, her arms crossed over her chest.

Butcher and Lottie didn't answer.

"Here." Lottie rolled out a medical kit, pulling a small scalpel free. "Check the infection."

Butcher pressed the knife against Zero's wrist, making a tiny cut in the skin. It oozed the dark, putrid blood.

"Fuck, it's gotta go." He examined the arm while Lottie tried to make Zero comfortable. "The infection's spreading."

"How high?"

He ran tiny pricks up Zero's arm, each oozing the dark liquid. Two inches below Zero's elbow, the blood flowed red for the first time.

"Here," Butcher declared, pulling a sharpie out of his pocket, and making a mark a finger width above the cut. "We'll have to do it here to ensure there's no contamination."

Lottie silently pulled the tourniquet free, handing Butcher a clean sheet to settle under Zero's arm, laying out bandages, equipment, and the like at the ready.

"We're gonna need a fire," Butcher directed. "We need to cauterize the wound, otherwise he'll bleed out."

Wrath gave me a squeeze, then moved to the side of the road to build a bonfire, Pope assisting.

Ghost, Switch and Ava set up a perimeter.

"Audrey, Ellie, we need the backseat of the SUV cleared out. Move the stuff to the trucks or wherever but we need somewhere flat to transport him."

"On it," Audrey said, moving immediately as directed.

They moved about, setting up the makeshift surgery while the fire built.

"Texas, Jo, you're gonna have to keep him still. I need one of you on his chest, the other on his legs." She looked at me. "Kate, You're on his arm. You need to keep him calm."

I swallowed, nodding, and moving to take up my position. He seemed out of it, his eyes staring at the sky, his skin still that nasty grey.

Butcher finished tying off the second tourniquet. He'd wrapped one strap just above the line, another sat on the first red cut, preventing further infection from the bite.

Butcher and Lottie shifted, stripping off their bloody battle clothes and changing. They scrubbed themselves with hot water, removing blood and dirt then scrubbed their hands with alcohol.

Butcher retrieved two machete from the SUV and moved to the fire, dowsing both blades with alcohol before passing one off to Ava, both of them holding the metal in the heat.

I looked down at Zero. "You're gonna be fine," I said, hoping it was the truth. "We'll get you sorted."

Lottie returned, shifting me slightly to make room. She may be a vet, but I'd long ago learned that she considered humans nothing but big animals. She'd applied her training to us more than once when Blair and Aella were stuck helping someone else.

"Drip is in," she said, holding the fluid line high. "Gonna need a blood transfusion though."

Butcher returned, the knife sterilised. "We don't have any blood."

"We can do a direct fusion if you link me up in the truck. I'm O negative." Lottie handed me the IV. "Hold it high, keep him still."

She pulled a needle from her pocket, ripping the lid off and testing it for bubbles before sticking it into Zero's wrist. She snatched a stick from the ground, pressing it between Zero's teeth.

"Morphine's in. Give him five and we're good." She moved around to the infected arm, placing her gloved hands on Zero's wrecked wrist.

"Ready."

Butcher looked down at Zero. "I'm sorry, brother."

With an almighty heave, he cut right across the marked line. Under me, Zero bucked, a soul-destroying scream bursting from his lips.

"One more," Butcher called jerking the machete free of the bone. "Hold him."

He bucked under Texas and Jo, attempting to thrash, attempting to escape.

"Now!" Jo screamed, barely holding his legs. "Hurry!"

Butcher's blade slashed down again, Zero's arm tossed away by Lottie. Ava passed the spare machete to Butcher, the man leaning down to press the hot blade to the rendered flesh. The cooked flesh mixed with blood, the smell putrid.

Zero screamed again, then collapsed, his eyes rolling into the back of his head, the stick falling to the ground.

"Thank God," Lottie muttered as she checked Zero's vitals. "Small mercy."

Butcher pulled the blade free, checking the wound. "Small bleed, gonna need to go again."

Lottie shifted into the space he left, holding Zero's shoulder down with her knees, her hands pressed to the arm to keep it in place.

Butcher lay the hot metal against the skin again briefly.

It wasn't how I imagined it would be. Laying heat on the wound until it charred completely. Instead, it was like little presses, just enough seal the flesh.

"Is he doing it right?" I asked Lottie, unable to help myself.

"Uh-huh," Lottie answered her hands working scissors to cut the clothing from Zero's body. "You don't want to burn the skin, that'll cause its own issue. You just want to make sure that no blood is moving about, but not so much that you burn healthy tissue." She looked up, her face pale but determined. "Pass me that bottle."

I lifted the clear alcohol, handing it over. Lottie waited for

Butcher's nod then doused Zero's arm in the liquid. He woke, screaming in pain, fighting once again before collapsing back into unconsciousness.

Thank God.

They dressed the wound, removing the tourniquet and giving Zero a shot of antibiotics. Lottie quickly checked his body, scrubbing it clean of blood with brisk, efficient movements. Butcher focussed on his vitals, monitoring the patient.

"We need to move him."

It took four men to lift him up and into the back of the SUV. Lottie climbed in, setting his head in her lap. They covered him with blankets to prevent against shock. Butcher worked quickly setting up a vein to vein blood transfusion between Lottie and Zero.

"You good?"

She nodded. "Just get us to the safe house. Quickly."

Wrath pressed a quick kiss to my mouth. "Stay with Texas."

Our party split. Wrath leading the SUV containing Butcher, Zero and Lottie, with Switch riding as support to get to the next overnight safe house. Audrey, Pope, Texas, Jo, Ava, Ghost, Runner, Ellie, and I would follow—stopping to plant Audrey's transmitters and fill the tanks at the rest stops.

"We need to change," Ava ordered, tossing a bag down. "Burn the clothing."

We removed every inch, throwing the bloody items on the fire to burn the bastard's blood, then scrubbed down using water Pope and Wrath had heated.

We checked each other over, modesty discarded for survival. Apart from some minor scratches and bruising, of which Ava had a major black eye, we were all clear.

We dressed quickly and I climbed into the truck beside Texas, Ellie on my other side, both of us curling into each other as he started the engine.

Pope, Ava, Runner and Ghost rode the bikes, Jo driving the other tanker, Audrey riding with her. We weren't taking any chances this time.

As we bumped along the road, the adrenaline began to wear off, my eyes drifting close. I shot up with a start but immediately crashed, my eyes heavy.

"It's okay," Ellie told me, patting my back. "I'll take first watch. We'll be with the others soon."

With that permission, I gave in, letting sleep take me.

Chapter Nine

Wrath

My bike sputtered to a halt a kilometre from the safe house. I parked it on the side of the road, making a mental note of the landscape around. I'd have to come back that night with fuel.

Mount Nombinnie was our stop for tonight. A safe house located four hours from the Murrumbidgee River, it'd put plenty of distance between us and the bastards—and give us a safe place to hole up for a few days while Zero recovered.

The SUV slowed, and I jumped in, gesturing at the dirt road. "Just keep following this until it forks then take the right. Our destination is the fortified farmhouse at the top of the hill."

The farmhouse had been built decades before and added to by generations. Originally built on the top of the hill to take advantage of the views, it now provided a perfect vantage point for its occupants.

"Who are the owners?" Lottie asked from the back seat. "Are they club members?"

"Relatives. Where we went one percent, they went hooah," Butcher replied.

There was a pause. "I have no idea what that means."

"They're all ex-military," I answered, watching the fields for movement. Switch rode behind, babying his own bike to the safe house.

The rest of our party were likely hours behind, needing to stop to set up the transmitters and refuel some of the safety points in between. Ghost and Runner had travelled this road before, and I had no doubt they'd keep my woman safe. My focus had to be on Zero.

We bumped up and down the dirt drive, rocks and dirt crunching under our tyres as we came to the thick steel gates of the farmhouse.

Two men stood on a parapet at the top of the wall, guns pointed at us.

I wound down my window, poking my head out. "You wanna drop those guns and let us in?" I called giving Jason and Vince a head lift. "We got an injured guy here."

"Wrath!" Jason called, giving me a wave. "Good to see you mate." He turned, gesturing at the gatekeepers. "Open her up, boys."

The sound of metal sliding against metal filled the air, a moment later one of the giant gates swung open, two guys running out to point weapons down the road as we drove in.

"They always like this?" Butcher asked quietly as we pulled in.

"No." I looked around. "This level of protection is new."

It'd been at least two months since I'd been through here. Most of that time had been spent working my way to the other clubs, delivering Shield, our National President's orders. The increased risk from militia groups, the virus, food and fuel shortages, and slavers—not to mention bastards—had forced Shield's hand. He'd ordered all our chapters back to three clubs—the compound down in Adaminaby, the Bunker at Cunnamulla that served as a halfway point to the final destination, the Plantation up at Lake Proserpine.

In the before, a clear route from one to the other would take twenty-four hours. In the after, I'd planned for the drive from Adaminaby to Cunnamulla to take at least three days. With Zero's injury, I'd have to reconsider that timeline.

Butcher parked where directed, and we piled out. Switch came around, having cruised in beside us, immediately moving to open the door and assist in pulling Zero free of the vehicle.

"Wait!" a voice called over the yard. A woman pushed a makeshift bed our way. "Put him on here."

We carefully unloaded Zero, then rushed him through the yard to their infirmary. It wasn't as well-stocked as the compound but it would do for the moment.

Lottie and Butcher got to work, both looking exhausted but determined as they set up fluids, recleaned and checked the wound, administered antibiotics, and made Zero as comfortable as possible.

Seeing he was in good hands, I left, Switch following closely, his face tight.

"What's up?" I asked him.

"Never seen anything like it." He shook his head. "That was fucked up."

"Yeah."

The first time I'd encountered a bastard had been outside the Plantation, the Nameless Soul strong hold up in Queensland, about eight months before. Me and two other guys had been hunting deer. Deer were introduced in Australia by white guys with no fucking sense of environmental preservation back in the late nineteen-hundreds. In the before, they'd been labelled pests, in the after they were a food source.

We'd been tracking a herd, hoping to find their feeding grounds, and set up a blind nearby. Instead, we'd found their watering hole, a small creek that trailed through some lush undergrowth.

We'd stumbled across it, bending to drink when a woman had appeared on the other side of the creek. She'd been wearing the torn remains of a military uniform—camo pants and what remained of a dusty, sand coloured shirt. Her hair had been a rat's nest, filthy with dirt, leaves and sticks. She was missing one boot, the other untied but still on. Her face had been scratched to pieces, the rest of her not much better.

Her fingers had been curled, manipulated as if her hands were arthritic or broken. Blood had been oozing from a new cut in her arm, the liquid thick and black. She'd tilted her head at us, eyes bright and clear, no signs she wasn't human.

"You okay, love?" Bear had asked, shifting his weapon to his back, and moving to cross the creek.

That's when she'd pounced. Jumping across the creek to hit Bear head-on, knocking them both to the ground. She bit him, tearing into the flesh at his throat with teeth and hands.

The young prospect with us, Wall, he'd leapt forward, knife in hand, stabbing her in the side as she'd continue to carve into Bear's throat.

A second had appeared out of the tree line, another woman. She also wore camos, hers in worse shape than the original woman. I'd shot her, once in the leg. Hoping to incapacitate her enough to get her back to camp for questioning.

Instead, she'd charged ahead, almost as if she were unaware of the damage to her thigh. I'd fired again, hitting her chest then her head. She'd fallen after that, dead.

The prospect had killed the other one, but Bear had been in a bad shape. We'd carried him back to the Plantation. It'd been hours later when the fever had ravaged his body and his blood had turned black that we'd realised something wasn't right.

Within twenty-four hours he'd started attacking brothers, rampaging through the infirmary, swiping, and gnashing at anyone in his way. We'd put him down, a bullet between the eyes. It still haunted me.

"Yo, Wrath."

I stopped, shifting to see Farmer come up behind us.

Like many in the after, he no longer went by the name his parents had bestowed upon him. In the after, surnames meant nothing, carrying no weight or value. Most of the club had defaulted to their road names, but a few insisted on changes.

Farmer, contrary to his name, wasn't a farmer. No one quite knew where Farmer had picked up his name, but it had stuck. I'd always assumed it was because the guy looked like a rancher, big-boned, home fed, barrel-chested. His skin tanned, his hair bleached by the sun.

I waited for him to join us. He fell in beside me, shaking his head. "Your kid is lucky to be alive."

"Butcher and the girl, Lottie, they did all the work."

"Good thing. Gonna be hell for him though." Farmer shook his head. "Won't ride a bike again."

In the before that statement wouldn't have been true. I'd been to rallies and there'd been plenty of amputee bikers with modified kit riding about. But in the after, it'd be harder. I doubted we'd be able to find him a prosthetic, and even if we did, his bike would have to undergo major modifications to enable him to ride. Modifications that I doubted we had the equipment or parts to achieve.

"Fucked up," I agreed.

We headed out to the yard, Farmer pointing at the new build going on around us.

"We're seeing an increase in bastard movement in this area. Not to mention fuckwit militia and wanna be army boys looking to fuck us over." He smirked, arms crossing over his chest. "They're learning not to come this way."

From what I'd gathered over the years, Farmer was ex-special ops. His gang of men had retired a few years before the virus had begun to ravage civilization. The guy was a prepper and had bailed out of society early, buying up land and settling in this area. He was club adjacent, his woman was Shield's sister, which meant they got club protection—even if they didn't want it.

"New towers." He gestured at the wooden buildings under construction around the courtyard. "Gonna make the fence higher too."

"Higher?" Switch asked, raising an eyebrow. "But the bastards can't climb."

The virus had certain strains of rabies running through it, in addition to the other DNA strands. Like rabies, it mutated muscle functions, twisting and paralysing some parts, in particular hands and toes. Bastards would swipe, they couldn't claw. Which meant climbing shit like a fence was virtually impossible.

"It's to keep the militia out." Farmer tucked his hands into his pockets, pausing in the middle of the courtyard. "The higher they have to climb, the longer we have to pick them off and prevent them from getting in." He nodded at the front of the yard where men were working to fortify the existing fence.

"We're digging down, gonna go five feet down into the

ground and fill the bitch with concrete. They can ram a truck into the fucker and she'll stand."

"Smart." I looked around the yard, taking a quick count. "You've recruited more boys."

"Friends escaping cities." He shook his head. "We've got a crew out on hunting duty, they're due back today, otherwise I'd offer you their beds. We're working on building a new bunkhouse out back, but at the moment all I have to offer you is the barn or some tents."

I clapped him on the shoulder. "The barn'll be fine. We're not fancy."

He grinned. "How many you expecting?"

"Tell your men to be on the lookout for a few bikes and two tankers. There'll be women in our party."

Farmer raised an eyebrow in question.

"You'll see." I looked at Switch. "Let's go get our shit set up in the barn."

I paused, looking back at Farmer. "Whip pass through here?"

He shook his head. "Ain't seen anyone through here for a good two weeks. Last was a guy coming from Queensland. Said he was headed over to Bathurst to touch base with a club out that way."

I nodded, my mouth thinning. "Thanks."

Switch and I headed to the barn, Switch sending me side glances as we moved.

"What?" I asked, scoping out the inside. There were eight stalls, six of which were occupied by horses or cows. The two at the back were free, though we'd disturbed a pair of napping barn cats. They hissed at us as they scattered.

"Whip should have passed through, right?"

"Maybe." I didn't like it either. "He could have heard word

of the horde and decided to reroute."

"Hope so."

So did I.

Chapter Ten

Kate

It was late when we finally drove up the hill towards the fortified farmhouse. The sun had set about half an hour ago, putting me on edge.

Ellie's head was on my shoulder, her body bouncing and swaying as the truck bumped along the road, headed up to the farmhouse. I'd woken a few hours ago, and she'd fallen asleep shortly after. Our adrenaline had worn off, leaving us feeling bruised and exhausted.

Though I had no doubt Audrey would want to debrief once we got up to the farmhouse. At every stop, while she set up the transmitters, Ghost, Pope and Ava working to secure the area or pump fuel into carefully hidden tanks, I'd seen her trying to talk to Ghost, obviously seeking more information.

A light flashed on us from the wall, the spotlight bright and nearly blinding.

"Fuck!" Texas barked, raising an arm to block the bright light. "What the fuck is this shit?"

The light switched off, and we continued to bump along, Ellie now awake but silent beside me.

"You okay?" I asked quietly.

"Maybe."

I felt that response in my soul.

At the crest of the hill a giant gate opened, men with weapons streaming out, taking position on either side of the fence. A man stood in the middle of the yard, waving us in.

"Guess we can safely assume they made it," Texas muttered, pulling into the yard, and following the man as he directed them to a park.

The gates shut behind us, Ava, Pope and Ghost safely inside, the other tanker rolling to a stop beside ours. I glanced over, already Audrey was jumping out, her hands moving excitedly as she chattered to Jo. Jo looked exhausted, her face drawn and frustrated.

I quickly followed Ellie as she jumped from the cab, moving across to them.

"Zombies!" Audrey yelled, spotting us. "Motherfucking zombies!"

Jo shifted, moving away from Audrey, and heading for the bikes where Ava, Ghost and Pope stood, quietly chatting.

"Not zombies," Wrath corrected Audrey. He emerged from the shadows around us.

God, I wanted him to reach for me. To kiss me. I wanted him to pull me into his arms and hold me tight. I ached for it, for the reassurance that we were alive.

His gaze focussed on me but he kept his distance as he answered Audrey.

"Bastards. They're not dead. They can bleed out. They can deteriorate, starve, die. They're alive, humans trapped inside the body of a rabid animal. Their minds destroyed; their bodies broken."

Audrey paused, tilting her head to one side. "So, the virus is like a parasite, taking over the host?"

Wrath shrugged. "Don't know. Don't really care to be honest. Just know the kindest thing is to put the bastards down."

I sucked in a breath. "Zero?"

"Alive. Looks like they stopped the infection. But we just gotta wait and see."

I nodded.

"Welcome!" a big voice boomed from the rear of the vehicles.

We all turned, a big man in faded jeans and a plaid shirt stood grinning as he eyed the tankers. "I see you're bringing us a bounty, friends."

"Guys, this is Farmer, our host."

Wrath introduced us and Ava quickly sized up the man. "You're ex-military."

He grinned. "So are you."

She crossed her arms over her chest, narrowing her eyes on him. She didn't say anything further, just watched him with suspicion.

"We've got hot showers and clean clothes awaiting you. Wrath and Switch have set up beds for you, though you'll be in the barn, my apologies for that." He tapped the side of the tankers. "Go change. Food will be waiting. I expect this is quite the story."

As we headed to the bathhouse, a call went up from the wall.

"Hunting party's returning!"

"Looks like you'll get fresh meat tonight," Farmer said with a nod to the tower. "Looks like you guys are already a lucky charm."

Inside the bathhouse were individual stalls, each lockable.

Wrath and Switch, having already showered and changed,

stood guard. Perhaps it was overkill, considering we were amongst friends. But I was grateful for the extra protection. Being naked and vulnerable wasn't something I wished to experience.

"Fuck this is good!" Pope yelled as the sound of spray hitting tiles echoed through the room. "Bloody missed this."

"How can you have missed this? The barge had a fucking shower," Audrey called back.

"Shut your mouth and let me enjoy this, woman!"

I hid a smile, placing my filthy clothes in the bag provided and stepping under the hot spray. I washed my hair, dirt and dust washing down the drain.

Behind me, my door opened, and I yelped, my mouth opening to scream.

Wrath grinned, pressing a finger to his lips.

"You scared me," I whispered as he shut the door, locking it once more.

"Sorry." He stripped off his clothes, placing them on the small bench provided. Naked, his cock hard and heavy, he stepped under the showerhead, capturing me, pulling me to him, kissing me with a ferocity I'd never experienced.

"Ghost owed me one," he murmured against my lips. "We're good for at least ten minutes."

His hands roved my body, as hungry and needy as I felt. The water added a layer of sensation, pouring over me.

Wrath dropped to his knees, his hands gently pushing me back until I hit the tiles, the cool of them adding another layer to this experience.

"Gotta be quiet," he whispered, gently guiding my legs open.

I nodded. Wrath's fingers slid up my legs, teasing the warmed skin. Water slicked down his body, emphasising the planes and hollows, dips, and curves. He was majesty and muscle, glory and grunt. His body carved by God and approved by the devil.

His cock jutted out, proud and erect. I wanted to touch him and reached out to pull him up but he shifted shaking his head.

"Keep your hands against the wall."

I pressed my palms against the cool tile, desperate to see what followed.

Wrath's hair stuck to his forehead, dark with water. He looked younger at this moment. The hard lines he normally wore had faded, leaving behind naked desire.

His hands trailed up my inner thighs, finding my pussy. Gently, he tangled fingers in my curls, parting my lips. He leaned forward, sending me a filthy look before his mouth pressed hot against my core.

I jumped, the sensation still new and incredibly erotic.

Would I ever get used to this? To the need, the hunger, the heat?

I hoped not.

He murmured something I couldn't hear over the sound of the shower. But I felt it, felt his approval as he tasted me, his mouth demanding. He teased and taunted, drawing from me panting gasps and barely smothered moans.

Around us, the showers slowly turned off, the sounds of people moving about as they dried and changed added to my need.

I want to come.

My hand lifted of its own accord, shifting to fist his hair, directing his mouth to where I needed it most.

He chuckled, obliging me. He reached up, turning the water off but not moving as he continued to lick and suck. His hands massaging my arse, his beard scraping against my most sensitive skin.

Sensations flowed until I couldn't distinguish one from another, until I was balanced on a precipice, willing to dive over.

Wrath lifted, boosting my body up the wall, his hands holding me until only my toes touched the floor. His mouth was ravenous, stroking, sucking, licking.

Once, twice, three times he teased my clit, his clever tongue applying more and more pressure until I shattered.

My pussy flooded and he made a growl of approval as I clenched, pleasure exploding out, sizzling through every vein and nerve. Every atom in my body branded with his name.

I must have made a noise or cried out because a moment later my feet touched the ground and Wrath was surging up, gathering my hands together and pressing them above me, his cock hard and hot against the soft skin of my belly.

"Tell them to fuck off," he ordered, face fierce.

"Who—?"

"You okay in there Kate?" Audrey asked, knocking on the door. "Did you slip?"

My wide, startled eyes met Wrath's. Amusement danced in their depths, mingled with desire. I loved that look on him. Loved that he looked at me as if I were his world.

Am I? Or is this just lust?

God, I hated the uncertainty.

"Fine," I replied, biting my lip as Wrath began to grind his cock against me.

"You sure?"

"Uh-huh. Just, umm...." I wracked my brain, trying to think of an convenient excuse. "I found a cut. I need to clean it."

"Okay. You want me to bring some antiseptic?"

Wrath dropped one hand, fisting his cock. Wet slicked my

thighs, my need rising once again.

"No," I replied, desperate. "I'm all good."

"Okay, hun. Don't be too long. Dinner is coming."

I distantly heard her shuffle out but no longer cared. All my energy centred on Wrath.

"Gonna come all over these pretty tits," he barked, dropping his head to capture one nipple between his lips. I arched, unable to do more as his hand kept me pinned to the tiles, his mouth worshipping my breasts while he violently fisted his cock.

He left my nipple, coming up to press his lips to my ear. "Do you realise how long I've waited for this moment, Sunshine?" he asked harshly. "Years of fisting my fucking cock. Years of imagining you pink and wet under me. Years of wondering what colour your pretty nipples would be. Would your cunt taste like sunshine or spice? Would you scream or sigh? Fucking years, Kate. Years of nothing but filthy fantasies that I knew would forever go unsatisfied."

He shifted, pushing me down. I moved, dropping gently to my knees, hands bracing on his thighs, looking up to find him devouring me with his gaze. Brutal, raw desire etched across every line of his body.

"Every moment with you is torture," he said hoarsely. His hand fisted his cock, violently tugging, jerking, twisting. "Every moment knowing I could have had this years ago. Knowing I should have played my hand. Fucking slices me, Kate. I'm being eaten alive by regret."

I rose up slightly, my hands moving to cup my breasts, looking up at him, giving him the only thing I could in this moment.

"Come on me, Wrath. Brand me. Make me yours."

He groaned, jerking his cock faster until his hot release hit my breasts, my neck, my chin. I didn't look away, didn't shy from the almost furious need that still burned in him. Instead, I let him see how much I loved it. How much I wanted it. How much I gloried in him and this moment.

"Fuck." He dropped down, gathering me into his chest, heedless of getting his release over himself. "You're fucking beautiful decorated in me, Kate."

I grinned, letting him tilt my head up. His thumb rubbed across my chin, spreading a little of his cum across my lips. I licked, tasting his release, the salt fuelling my need no less urgent now.

"Let's get you cleaned up," he told me, his eyes dark. "We'll be missed."

He lifted us up and helped me clean him from my body.

As I watched him wash, I had a feeling no matter how much I tried, I'd be unable to clean him or this moment from my soul.

And I had no idea how I felt about that.

Chapter Eleven

Wrath

Ghost, hair damp, stood outside the shower block as we existed. Kate blushed, avoiding looking his way. Behind me, I could hear Switch singing in the shower. Kid had a fucking terrible singing voice but made up for it with enthusiasm.

"All good?" I asked, pausing by Ghost.

He nodded then inclined his head towards the main house. "Dinner's on."

I reached out, wrapping an arm around Kate, pulling her into my side as we walked towards the house.

"Are we official now?" she asked, her voice low.

That question felt like a sucker punch to the gut. "You don't wanna be?"

She smiled up at me. "No, I do. I just wanted to double-check that you were okay with us being open about it."

"Waited a long fucking time, Kate. Not gonna hide." I stopped us in the middle of the yard, turning her until her chest pressed against mine.

"We're in this, Sunshine. There's no going back. I'm not letting you go again."

She blew out a breath. "I want this. A lot."

I grinned, bringing her in, kissing her pretty lips. "Good."

We continued to the farmhouse; the darkness quite complete. I found Ava and Pope outside looking furious.

"I told them," Ava raged when she saw us. "I fucking told them."

I lifted an eyebrow at Pope in question but he was watching Kate.

"Ava, take Kate to the barn," Pope told her. "Wrath and I will deal with this."

"Deal with what?" Kate asked, her arm tightening around me.

"I'll explain in the barn," Ava said.

"No." Kate stood her ground. She let go of me, crossing her arms. "Tell me."

Pope and Ava exchanged a look. Unease slid down my back, my hand itched to pull the weapon from my holster.

"Kate," Ava finally said, looking back at her, her face grim. "Your father's here."

She startled, her body jerking. I reached for her but she pulled back, her hands coming up, her head shaking as denials fell from her lips.

"N-n-no, he's dead. Th-that's i-i-impossible."

If he isn't then he will be.

Years before, one night when we'd been at her mother's grave, Kate had explained why she sometimes stuttered. She'd been born with it, and while she'd worked hard for many years to master her speech, fear, stress and anxiety often got the better of her.

I'd noticed it when she'd been growing up, but had never paid mind to it until that night. Her speech patterns were slightly slower and more deliberate than other people as if the words her mouth crafted carried that much more weight.

Her stuttering statement set off a roar within me.

He's not gonna fucking touch her.

"Where is he?" I asked, moving to step around Pope.

"Inside. He was with the hunting party. Texas and Runner and dealing with him and Farmer."

I opened the door, a red haze taking over my vision.

Gus was a man who had been willing to trade and sell women in exchange for his own hide. He had no honour, no right to life after that act.

I had no doubt that he'd have sold Kate in a heartbeat. His every decision concerning his daughter had resulted in her pain and trauma. Years of neglect, allowing his wife—Kate's stepmother—to hurl abuse both verbal and physical upon her. He'd ripped opportunities out from under her, withheld her inheritance.

He'd been the reason Ice had never disclosed his relationship to Kate. My gut knew it. If he'd known about that relationship, he'd have tried to break it. Tried to break Ice the same way he'd broken his other children, attempting to either shatter them into a million pieces or mould them to his will.

But Kate was a diamond, forged under immense pressure, emerging unbroken and more beautiful than he could ever understand.

Where once I'd had no right to go against my president, no ability to protect her from him or his old lady, today I did. Today, at this moment, Gus no longer had the protection of the club. He was nothing but a traitor—to his blood, to his club, to our brotherhood.

He's going to die.

I tore through the house, heading for the main dining room, my hand automatically pulling a knife free. The hilt sat in the palm of my hand, heavy, the weight familiar.

One word and I was ready to gut the bastard.

"Ah, here he is!" Gus boomed, his arms spreading in welcome as I entered the room. "The prodigal son. He'll help me get this all straightened out."

I crossed the room, not holding back as I punched him square in the face, his nose making a satisfying crunch under my knuckles, blood spurting as he doubled over.

Ghost, Runner and Texas immediately took my back as Farmer's men crowded in, voices raised, women and children scattering.

"That's for Kate," I spat, watching in satisfaction as he wheezed. "The next one will be for the club."

"Stand down." Farmer waded in, bridging the gap between me and the fucker. "Let's talk this out."

"You know, I told you guys to just put a bullet in the fucker," Ava said from the doorway, leaning against it and watching with a bored expression as Gus struggled to his feet. "Cockroaches always survive."

Kate pushed passed, coming to me then looking over at Gus.

"Ah." Gus wiped at his nose, sending her a bloody grin. "I see ye've brought me daughter as well. How nice. We can have ourselves a wee reunion."

Farmer frowned, looking from Gus to us and back. "Jerry? What the fuck?"

"That isn't Jerry," Runner spat. "That's our ex-President. The fuckwit was trafficking women. Selling them to the militia and slavers."

Farmer's face turned to stone but I ignored him, focussing in on Kate. She stared at Gus, her fists clenching and unclenching. No one moved as Gus straightened, his arms opening once again.

"Ye'd punch a man for protecting his family?"

"Fuck you," Kate bit out, deliberate, and slow but no less deadly. "Y-y-you s-sell w-w-women. You're a p-p-piece of sh-sh-shit."

He dropped his arms, his expression cold as ice. "And ye're nothing but a mistake. Some spunk I dropped in an ungrateful cunt. I shudda taken care of ye years ago. Like me wife, God rest her soul, told me."

Heat raged through me, but I waited, watching for my moment. Gus had been here for God knew how long, weeks perhaps, filling their minds with whispered lies.

But then men around him were shifting, their expressions growing closed. It was in the way they moved back, slowly creating space between themselves and Gus.

Dig your grave. Dig it deep.

"My m-m-mother deserved better than the l-l-likes of you!" Kate bit out. "She was a g-g-g-goddamned s-s-saint."

"Ye mother wasn't nothing but a warm hole," Gus retorted, blood dripping from his chin to pool on the floor. "Only decent thing she ever did was die." He laughed. "Mama saw to that."

Kate moved, quicker than a flash she had her gun out and pointed at him. Men and women scattered, but Kate stared down her father, her expression deadly.

Gus rolled his eyes. "Ye're too much of a pussy to pull that trigger."

"S-s-say it again," she demanded, fury reddening her cheeks. "D-d-did you k-k-kill my m-mother?"

Gus laughed. "Weren't no drunk driver."

And just like that, he moved, reaching for the gun laying on the table beside him.

A gun fired. One-shot, straight to his chest.

For a beat the room was still, Gus blinking at his daughter in surprise, his hand still stretched out toward the table. He looked down at his chest, his hand coming up to touch the hole. Blood poured freely, soaking his shirt.

"Well, fuck me." He toppled over, falling to the floor, blood bubbles rasping from his mouth as he took his last breath.

As men moved to surround him, Kate turned to Farmer, handing him her gun.

"S-s-sorry about y-y-your floor," she said calmly, her words still stuttering but her expression peaceful.

"Sorry for your loss," Farmer replied, accepting her weapon. "If you hadn't done it, I would have."

She nodded and turned to me.

"Wrath?"

"Here, Sunshine."

She blinked up at me, her eyes wide and mouth pinched. "P-p-promise you'll send word of t-t-this to Ice?"

"On my life," I agreed. I took a step closer to her. Behind her, Farmer handed her weapon to Ghost.

"Good."

And with that her eyes rolled into the back of her head, her body falling like dead weight to the floor.

I caught her, scooping her up and lowering to the floor. Behind me, a declaration was made.

"He's dead."

Ava dropped beside me, Runner on Kate's other side.

"Shit." She pressed fingers to Kate's neck, her lips moving as she counted the beats. "She's okay. Just a faint."

"Better take her to the infirmary."

I lifted my woman, hefting her into my arms and turning for the door. I paused in the entry, turning back to Farmer.

"We gonna have an issue?"

He shook his head, raising his hands. "This is the after, brother. And your club is family. If this piece of shit betrayed not only your woman but your club, then far as I'm concerned, he's better off dead."

Good.

On the walk over, Ava dogged my heels, her little huffs sounding angry.

"What?" I finally barked.

"They should have just put a fucking bullet in his head."

Silently I agreed. No matter that he deserved it, this was a stain that Kate would wear on her soul forever.

"She's gonna hate herself."

"Nah." Ava waved a hand. "Kate's a fucking badass. She's done dirty jobs in the after. Even helped me bury the bodies. Said they'd make good compost in a year or three."

I barked out a laugh, imagining my Sunshine girl as a bloodthirsty animal. The visual was next to impossible.

Ava stopped me with a hand on my arm.

"She's stronger than you assume," she told me, her eyes searching my face. "But don't think because her backbone is made of steel that her heart isn't tender. You have to respect the steel and protect the heart."

I nodded, committing the advice to memory.

"Now go." Ava waved me off. "Ghost will no doubt be following shortly and I'd really like to spend one night without a tail."

I grinned. "Sorry to tell you, won't be tonight."

"He's behind me, isn't he?"
I laughed, turning to walk into the infirmary.

87

Chapter Twelve

Kate

I woke to a dimmed room and the sound of a low moan.

I lay still, blinking at the unfamiliar ceiling, taking stock of my surroundings. The moan came again, followed by a rustling of material then a whispered reassurance.

"You're okay," I heard Lottie murmur. "You can have a little more pain relief in an hour. You've already had the maximum for today."

I turned my head, seeing Zero in the bed beside mine. His muscles clenched, his face pale and sweating as painful moans slipped free. I couldn't tell if he was awake or sleeping, but either way, the loss of his arm had to be excruciating.

"You're awake."

I twisted, looking to my other side. Wrath sat on a camp chair; his body leaned towards me as he grinned though worry floated in the depth of his blue eyes.

"You okay?" he asked, reaching out a hand to brush hair from my cheek.

I nodded, pushing to sit up. "Yeah, I'm fine." I stretched, testing my body for aches and pains. Apart from bone-deep weariness, I felt nothing.

"You remember what happened?"

The gun bucking under my hand, the blood pooling, spreading across Gus' chest, his surprised expression and shock that his own flesh and blood had done it. The grim satisfaction that I'd avenged my mother, destroyed the man who'd killed the person I loved most in the world.

"Yeah." I pushed off the bed, swinging my legs around and standing up. "I-I-I-I…." I paused, sucking in a breath and channelling decades of speech therapy to bounce my words and minimise my stuttering. "I'm not sorry."

I reached for my jacket, pulling it on as Wrath watched me, his face contemplative.

"What?" I asked, zipping up the jacket and tucking hands into my pockets.

"You're different."

I shrugged. "Aren't we all? The after doesn't allow us to be soft, Wrath. And my… and G-G-Gus beat it outta me long ago."

He stood, hands slipping to my biceps, curling around them, and gently pulling me close.

"Correction, he tried." Wrath raised a hand, cupping my jaw. "The after may force us to don spikes to protect our backs. But it also makes us appreciate what we have that much more."

I laughed. "You're being sentimental, Wrath. That's not like you."

He leaned forward kissing my cheek gently before shifting to place a hand on my back. "No one's going to punish you, Kate. He betrayed us and lied to Farmer. If you hadn't done it, Farmer would have."

I nodded, taking a deep breath as I straightened my shoulders.

"Guess we better go."

"We'll bring you a plate," he told Lottie, who was settling in beside Zero, a novel in her hands.

"Butcher said he'd bring one over." She lifted the novel. "Kate, they have a library. And they're willing to let us swap."

"Oh Lordy," I breathed, pressing a hand to my chest. "New books."

We grinned at each other before Lottie dropped her head, settling back in to begin reading. "Go." She waved us off dismissively. "We're good here."

Wrath guided me out of the clinic and across the large yard of the farm. The night was quiet except for the occasional cricket and the low hum of the large spotlights that lit the grounds.

"Solar," Wrath explained, catching me looking up at the lights. "No one can fuel generators anymore." His mouth twisted into a wry smile. "Well, no one except those of us with a biochemist on our payroll."

I chuckled, leaning into him. "Life finds a way."

He groaned, "You're still obsessed with Jurassic Park? Kate, we need to talk."

I chuckled. The farmhouse had three men standing around outside, two eating, the third on watch.

"Go on in," the watch guy said, nodding his head towards the door. "They're in the dining room."

Inside, Gus' body had been removed, the floor and wall scrubbed clean. Even the hole from where the bullet had passed through him and embedded into the wall had been patched over, the plaster still drying.

Farmer runs a tight ship.

The room was full of chairs, people eating from plates balanced on their laps. A long table was set against one wall, holding the remains of a self-serve dinner.

"You're here." A woman smoothly rose from beside Farmer, handing him her plate and opening her arms wide in greeting. "Hello, Kate."

"Mari." I met her halfway, wrapping my arms around her. "It's been a long time."

Years before she'd met Farmer, Mari had travelled with Shield, her brother, visiting the chapters. Shield was a good national president. He cared for his members, was tuned into the needs of the brothers and their women. When a brother or his family got sick, Shield made sure they had what they needed. When a brother passed, he'd be there, comforting his family, making sure they knew they'd be taken care of.

Mari was like that. All goodness and light. I'd known it had been a rough time for her when she'd fallen for Farmer. Shield had wanted her to stay in the club, but Farmer wasn't the kind of guy who could follow orders from another man—not after his experience in the military.

Mari stepped back, offering me a warm smile, her hands resting on my biceps as she gave them a gentle squeeze. "Your food's in the kitchen warming. I'll go get it. Grab a seat and something to drink. They're just about to start."

She waddled off, her slight belly bump leading the way.

"Five months," Farmer said noting the direction of my gaze. He looked worried. "She's over the morning sickness but tires easily."

"Women have birthed babies for millennia," Audrey said from her seat by the fire. The room had only candles and the massive fireplace lighting the space. "And we know so much more about pre- and post-natal health these days. Not to mention the advanced care, equipment and medicine." She lifted her glass, tilting it at Farmer. "You should ask Blair to come and help with the delivery if you don't already have a midwife or doctor here. She knows her shit."

Wrath and I found spare seats, dragging them over to join our small party, who were mingled with Farmer's crew. I remembered a few faces from years ago, but most of his people were new to me.

Mari returned, handing Wrath and I heaped plates of roast chicken, mash, and spring veggies.

"We're getting better at farming," she said with a laugh as she settled back beside Farmer. "But lord knows that we could use some pointers if you're staying around for a few days."

I glanced at Wrath, seeing him exchange a look with Runner and Ghost.

"If you'll have us, we'll stay until it's safe to transport Zero," Wrath finally said, lifting his fork and spearing a green bean.

"You're welcome as long as you'd like," Farmer replied, placing his plate on the ground, settling back with a large bottle of homebrew beer. "But I'll need some help with hunting if we're gonna keep you fed."

Our gathering nodded.

"Now, who wants to tell me about the fuel?"

Wrath looked to Runner and Ellie, who grinned.

Runner pulled Ellie a little tighter against him, giving her a little shake. "Ellie here is a biochemist. She's the brains behind the biofuel."

She blushed. "We're replenishing the pitstops along the way. But our goal is to hit Cunnamulla and stop for a month while we teach them."

"If they have the kit," Audrey added. "Might take longer if they don't have the right shit."

"And what do they need?" Farmer asked, leaning forward.

Ellie shrugged. "It depends on what crops they have. Soy, corn, depends. You can make biofuel out of a lot of things. The main issue is ensuring your equipment is correctly configured and what you're producing is clean enough to not break your engines."

"Tell me more."

As Ellie and Runner spoke, telling Farmer about the options for biofuel, I finished eating, listening with half an ear but mostly observing the surrounds.

Back at the university, we'd been wary of strangers, only occasionally making an approach when someone wandered into our little oasis. Sometimes it worked in our favour, providing us with information about the state of the world and the virus.

Other times, the individual had tried to take advantage of thirteen women. Ava had dealt with them, but I hadn't felt right leaving her alone to do it, neither had Jo. We'd helped, disposing of the bodies or just being Ava's silent observers, supporting her as she did what was necessary.

While we'd been isolated, it appeared that connected colonies of survivors had adopted new rituals. Rituals dealing with food and shared stories. It felt old, a return to a time before technology when entertainment relied on individuals retelling stories imprinted into their memory and news only passed from lips to ears.

Mari and a few of the gathered, cleared plates as Farmer spoke to our group. I rose, assisting, giving Wrath a reassuring smile as I collected the cutlery and plates of those nearest me.

They had blown out the kitchen, enlarged to include three wood-burning stoves, a giant fire oven, and a fully industrial sink. Some younger men were pumping water, heating it in a large pot over one of the stoves.

"Wow," I commented, handing my items off to Mari. "This is impressive."

She laughed, dropping the plates on the sink with the others. "Farmer knew we'd run out of gas and fuel. He wanted to make sure we weren't reduced to relying on a campfire."

An old man, wrinkled and a little bent, sat beside one of the stoves, feeding more wood into the belly. "Coffee and tea?" he asked.

"Thanks, Sam, I think they're about ready for it."

He nodded, then made shooing motions with his hands. "Go, the boys and I will serve."

Mari stopped me just outside the kitchen, in the small hall between that and the dining room.

"You're headed to the Plantation, aren't you?"

I nodded. "That's the goal."

She rubbed her stomach, a bittersweet smile on her face. "Wrath was the last nomad who's passed through. I know it's selfish, but could you take a letter for me?" She rested a hand on her belly. "Shield doesn't know about the baby. And I want him to know that he's going to be an uncle before it actually happens." She blinked back tears, her beautiful brown eyes swimming. "If he can't be here then at least he can know."

I swallowed, reminded that once again the after was a cruel life.

"Of course." I sucked in a breath. "Do you have an old camera around here? With film by any chance? Audrey knows how to print the photos if we can set up a darkroom."

She blinked. "Are you serious?"

I shrugged. "Yeah. If you'd like to try."

She threw herself at me, wrapping her arms tight. "Thank you! God, thank you!"

Mari pushed back, brushing tears from her cheeks, her smile dazzling. "I'll track one down. We'll make it happen."

Pleased I'd been able to give her this little piece of joy, we turned, moving to rejoin the gathering.

Chapter Thirteen

Kate

Back in the dining room, Farmer pulled Mari onto his lap, cupping her face.

"You okay?"

"Perfect," she beamed. "Hormones. You know how I am."

He chuckled, pressed a kiss to her forehead then looked back at Ellie. "What could we do to tempt you to stay here and help us set up our own facility?"

Ellie laughed, placing a hand on Runner's leg. "Nothing. That would be up to the Nameless Souls to decide."

Butcher returned from dropping off food to Lottie, a large container of Yana's cookies in hand. We shared them with the group, as Sam and the younger men brought out coffee and tea, and Runner, Wrath and Farmer attempted to work out logistics.

"Then it's settled," Farmer finally said sometime later. "When you return, we'll have the gear and product ready to go."

"It might be a while," Runner cautioned, holding a mug of coffee in one hand, one of Ellie's clasped in his other. "Depending on what we find at the other chapters and how long it takes them to get up and running. We might be months."

"But you'll return, and that's the main thing."

"Um, excuse me." Audrey raised a hand. "I don't mean to interrupt, but I feel that conversation might be at an end so, can I ask…." She placed her mug on the ground then linked her hands, index fingers pressed against her lips, head tipped down slightly as she paused. "What. The actual fuck. Were those things? Zombies? Motherfucking zombies?"

I blew out an amused sigh. We'd been lucky enough to have her wait this long.

"Bastards," Wrath corrected with a frown. "I told you earlier. They're not dead. They're just bastardised humans. The virus reducing them to desperate animals."

She waved a hand at him, brushing him off. "Yeah, I get that. Zombie, bastard, tom-ay-toe, tom-ah-toe." She leaned forward. "But explain it to me. The genesis. We heard *nothing* about those things at the College. Not one traveller mentioned them. Is this a new mutation?"

"Not sure," Farmer said, rubbing a hand across his brow. "They came from up north. First sighting was just after the cities went black."

I saw Ava stiffen, watching Farmer carefully.

Discreetly, I lifted my hands, signing, *you okay?*

She caught my signal and nodded once, sucking in a deep breath, then carefully wiping her face clear of all expression.

"But you guys knew about them?" Audrey looked to the Nameless Souls men. "You've seen them before?"

"Not this far south," Wrath replied with a shake of his head. "They've been keeping to the north of the state. We'll pass through their hunting grounds to get from Cunnamulla up to the Plantation."

"Hunting grounds?" Jo sat up, her eyes wide, face paling. "Did you say motherfucking hunting grounds?"

He nodded. "Did no one tell you?"

"Ah, that would be a fuck no." She looked at Texas. "Were you guys planning on telling us this shit or was it easier to leave us little women in the dark?"

He held up his hands in surrender. "Hey, don't blame me. The bastards are well known to us. I'd hazard a guess we assumed you knew."

"Not like that. When you said crazy, that they liked to kill or fuck, I was expecting like a meth addict kind of deal. You know, strong and fucking brutal. Not literal animals wanting to tear flesh from my body."

Ellie looked up at Runner. "You guys called the group that hit us a horde?"

"Yeah." He ran a hand over his chin, his scruff making a faint rasping noise. "They sometimes form packs. We're not sure if it's bastards who have the same strain of the virus, or if there's like a mother cluster or what. But sometimes they join together, tracking prey."

Audrey visibly shuddered. "It's *the Walking Dead*. We're in a fucking horror series."

"Audrey." Ava rubbed her temples. "Can we chill with the dramatics for a moment?"

"I'm just saying." She slapped the back of one hand against the palm of her other. "This year just keeps delivering. First, it was The Purge, then we lost Jules and Lilith, now it's–"

"The Purge?" A man to our left leaned forward, his gaze sharp. "You lost women to The Purge?"

"Maybe," I replied, my gut clenching with guilt and loss. "They went missing the night The Purge attacked our group.

We beat them back, but it changed everything for us."

A guy leaned forward, a man I didn't recognise. "Were they quality women?"

"Excuse me?" Ava said, hand shifting to palm her gun. "You wanna rephrase that question, buddy?"

He swallowed. "No offence meant. It's just…." he searched for the words. "The Purge, they're not taking on more women—not enough food. But they're collecting them for the Circus."

A shiver of unease went down my back.

"What the fuck is that?" Texas asked.

"It's a competition. Like a cage fight but to the ground. First one down is out. It's a round-robin competition. The final bout is to the death but the winner gets their choice of women. Then they move on to the next competition." The guy shrugged. "The Purge aren't abusing them—no one wants a fucked-up woman for a prize."

"But we saw their women," Ellie pointed out. "The women in the scouting parties were badly abused, naked, malnourished."

"That's the women The Purge are allowed to keep. If they're quality—good looking, breeding age, untouched or vaccinated, or a combination of those—they go into the ring as prizes."

"Fuck," Runner breathed, reaching out to wrap an arm around Ellie and pull her into his side. "This is fucked up."

"Word has it the Circus is being funded by some rich fucks hanging out in the Middle East. They've worked out how to rig a satellite feed for the fights."

"Money?"

"Nah, they're pushing oil this way."

Liquid gold.

"How do you know this?" Ava asked, still palming her gun.

Beside her, Ghost had his arms crossed over his chest, silently watching.

The man swallowed, grief lining his face. "My sister was taken. We tracked her to the Circus. Her husband went in to fight for her." He shook his head. "He didn't come out."

"And your sister?" Audrey asked.

"Won a few rounds later before I could get high enough in the bracket. No idea where she is now."

"What's the buy-in?" Ghost asked, his voice a rumble.

All eyes went to him in surprise.

"A woman or a truck of food." The guy shrugged. "If you barter a woman and win, you can take her home and get another of your choice. If you lose, she goes into the prize pool."

Ava rubbed her chin, glancing at Ghost. "You know where the next one of these is being held?"

"Last we heard they were on the move out to Dubbo."

"That's only four or five hours from here," Jo said.

"I've had a few men try their luck," Farmer told us. "The Circus has only been running for a few months."

"Any winners?"

"Two." He shrugged. "Both just wanted women. They wanted a chance at a family."

"And the women just came willingly?" Ava raised her eyebrow sceptically.

"No, but they're living on the property and have my protection until they decide what they want to do. We don't force women here."

"They're grateful for being rescued," Mari added. "If no one picks them after ten rounds, then they're offered to The Purge."

I shuddered, fear pooling as I thought of Jules and Lilith,

trapped in that slave ring.

"How many times can someone enter?" Runner asked.

"The reigning champion had a stable of about twenty women."

Ava's lips peeled back, baring her teeth. "They let women fight in these matches?"

There were chuckles.

"It's to the death," the man said, shaking his head. "You'd get wiped."

Ghost leaned forward, his leg a whisper from Ava's. "Way I see it we got two options. I can go, check it out, take Ava as she knows what her friends look like. We can meet back at Cunnamulla in a month."

"Second option?" Runner asked.

"We don't do anything and Ava goes it alone." He shot her a look. "You're gonna go, right?"

She raised her hands as if to say, *maybe*.

I knew her, she'd be going. If there was even a minuscule chance Jules and Lilith were alive, then she'd be there.

"The battles, when do they take place?"

"Every day for five days," Farmer answered. "There are two battles a day. You must win both to proceed. You get to the final day and it's a round-robin until the last man is standing."

"That's potentially twelve people you gotta drop before killing two people to win both Jules and Lilith." Audrey swallowed.

"There's a lot of desperate men out there."

I felt Wrath shift beside me, his gaze fixed on Ghost. "You sure, brother?"

Ghost didn't answer. He looked to Ava, deferring to her.

"If we find this Circus and Jules and Lilith aren't there, then we've only lost fuel and some time."

"But if they are?" Jo asked.

"Then I'll burn the entire thing down to get them back." Ava clenched her fists, pressing them into her thighs. "No woman left behind."

It'd been our promise to each other. An oath forged in blood and tears. And one that we'd failed to uphold when Lilith and Jules went missing.

"You'll have to fight," Farmer told Ghost. "And I don't have any spare food for you to barter. Not at this time of the year."

Spring after a hard winter. It had been unseasonably dry, and the frosts brutal. Crops were difficult to grow and maintain in those conditions. I expected a similar story at each of our stops along the way.

"He doesn't need your food," Ava told him. "He's got me."

"Abso-fucking-lutely not," Jo barked. "No fucking way, Ava. What if he loses?"

Ava cocked an eyebrow at Ghost, a hint of a challenging smirk on her lips. "You planning on losing?"

He gave her a dead stare.

"See?" She slapped hands on her thighs then rose from her seat. "Alright, I think it's bedtime. We'll need to get moving early tomorrow if Ghost and I are to make Dubbo by midday."

There were protests and arguments which Ava brushed off with a stubborn look and rolled eyes. Her decision had been made and neither God nor Audrey would sway her.

Wrath glanced at me. "You're not going to lodge a protest?"

I shrugged. "It wouldn't be worth the breath in my lungs. Ava's gonna do it anyway. We could hog-tie her and stake her to the ground in the middle of a maximum-security prison—she's still gonna escape and do what she thinks is right." I shot him a smile. "Besides, I don't disagree with her approach. I know Ghost's potential. He's not going to lose. And if he does, Ava will deal."

Wrath scratched his chin. "There's not much I'd put past that she-devil."

Chapter Fourteen

Wrath

We retired to the barn, but the complaints and arguments against Ava's plan continued.

We were settling down, Kate climbing into the sleeping bags I'd joined together while I helped Audrey and Jo set up their own area off to the side.

"Just wait," Audrey threatened, shooting Ava another glare. "Lottie's gonna freak."

"Lottie's gonna do what now?" Lottie asked from the hayloft ladder. Her mass of curls were limp, dark circles stark against her pale skin.

"What the fuck, Lottie?" Ava demanded, immediately moving to wrap an arm around her sister. "How much blood did you give him?"

"Not enough." She rubbed her eyes, allowing Ava to escort her to a pallet. "We'll need to give him more in the morning."

"Well you can find someone else," Ava barked, easing her sister down. "You're wrecked."

"Just tired." She sat, curling arms around her knees, laying her chin on them. "Now, what am I gonna freak about?"

"We have a lead on Jules and Lilith. But it's at a flesh market. Some kind of MMA hunger games shit. Ava wants her and Ghost to go." Audrey crossed her arms over her chest, her expression mulish. "We're protesting."

Lottie looked at her sister. "Reliable information?"

"Enough."

"You'll be careful?"

Ava grinned. "Am I ever?"

Lottie chuckled, lifting a hand, and limply waving it. "Go with my blessing then. Just make sure you come home."

Audrey spluttered for a moment then threw up her hands, spinning around. "That's fine. No one care about the risks or vulnerabilities. No one care that the percentage of this working in our favour is less than eight. No one care about the fact it's a one in twenty-two million shot that Jules and Lilith are even at the Circus."

"Audrey?" Pope called from where he lay on a pile of hay, one hand tucked behind his head, his eyes closed.

"What?"

"Go to bed."

She blustered for a moment, then sighed. "Fine."

She dropped beside Jo, crawling into her sleeping bag, and rolling over to give us her back.

I saw Kate watching Audrey expectantly. The woman didn't disappoint.

She pushed up, twisting back around. "Just know, Ava. I'm logging a formal protest. You get yourself killed and I *will* find a way to clone you just to bring you back and slap you for this."

"Noted," Ava replied, tucking Lottie into the sleeping bag. "Goodnight, Audrey."

With that, Audrey rolled over, huffing.

The hayloft may not have been the most comfortable place to sleep but it was warm and safe. A privilege in the after.

I crawled into the sleeping bag with Kate, pulling her drowsy body close.

"You okay, Sunshine?"

She nodded, her body settling against mine. "Just tired."

"Rest," I whispered against her hair, ignoring the aching of my cock as it responded to her nearness. "We'll deal with the world tomorrow."

As Kate grew heavy against me, slipping into sleep, and the sounds of those around us eased, I considered our future.

Life would never return to the familiarity of the before. It couldn't. Things were too broken, people too changed for it to return.

Though, having lived in a society built by men who hated guys like me, I couldn't say I found it a bad thing.

Nah, this new world suited me. No rules, not constrained by guys with shit for brains who didn't understand the idea of riding free.

What did worry me was Kate. All the women, really. Audrey had made good points about the danger Ava would face at the Circus. But I knew, perhaps more than most, that women in the after were treated worse than any other time.

When we thought fuel was a fleeting wish, Shield, our National President, had tasked me with pulling together the south chapters. The Compound, where the Adaminaby Chapter lived, was the largest property and most fortified of the southern chapters. I'd travelled to each chapter, finding them in various states of disarray

Some were faring well, working hard, and turning from soldiers into farmers. But it was the smaller chapters. The ones that had decided to stay—despite all efforts to get them to move—that suffered. Two chapters had been decimated, men slain, women and children captured by slavers or God knew who else.

With two male survivors, we'd tracked them to a holding pen, managing to break a few out. But we'd lost more. Swallowed up by man's greed and carnality.

I held Kate just a little closer, needing to feel her in my arms. Needing her weight, her smell, her presence to keep the demons at bay.

You could lose her.

The impossible thought detonated in my mind, ruining what little comfort I got from holding her.

Kate was more than just a woman or someone I loved. She was a hope. A dream. She was sunshine on my dark soul.

If anything happened to her….

My stomach clenched, my body reflexively shifting just a fraction to protect her. She mumbled a sleepy protest. I forced tension from my limbs, relaxing around her.

Our future would be made up of fights and death. I'd been living in purgatory for years, not knowing where she was or if she was safe. But nothing I'd felt during that time could compare to how I felt holding her in my arms. Having tasted her, having stroked, and kissed her—pain slashed through me, the bittersweet taste of longing regret.

I couldn't take back the moments I'd had with her. I wouldn't. But God, it made living that much harder, knowing I'd be destroyed if anything happened to her.

Nothing can ever happen to her.

Those words tattooed on my soul, burning into my flesh.

Kate was mine. And I'd burn the whole fucking world down

to protect her.

Chapter Fifteen

Kate

I woke to Wrath stroking my body, his hands unintentionally teasing the edge of my arousal. I lay in that perfect state between full consciousness and sleep, that twilight dream where everything felt both confusing and perfect.

"You have to get up," Wrath whispered in my ear, his breath warm.

"No," I whispered back, burrowing into him, letting his hands soothe. "This feels good."

He chuckled, continuing to stroke my skin slowly as the people around us began to move until finally I fully awoke to the new day.

I sighed, blinking my eyes open and offering Wrath a small smile. "Breakfast?"

"Coffee," he agreed.

We separated, moving out of the sleeping bags, and quickly changing. Everything was rolled up and repacked, ready for us to move at a moment's notice.

"How long are we staying here?" I asked, taking a quick sniff of my shirt as we walked to the farmhouse.

"Depends on Zero. At least a few days."

Audrey skipped up, linking her arm with mine. "You're thinking a washing day?"

"Yeah." I made a face. "At this rate, no one will want to kiss me but a bastard."

"Aww, don't say that," Audrey said, pulling me to a stop, her hands coming up to frame my face. "I'll kiss you."

She pulled me towards her, making exaggerated kiss lips and smooching sounds. I laughed, trying to fight her.

"Ohh, girl-on-girl." Pope made a whistling sound. "You won't see me complaining."

Audrey's hands dropped from my face, her back immediately going ramrod straight. She sent a withering glare his way. "Are you always so crass?"

He seemed to think it over, rubbing his chin. "Only around you."

She rolled her eyes, ignoring him and capturing my hand. "Come on, let's eat."

Inside the farmhouse was a decent spread. Fresh eggs and warm bread. An oat porridge with yoghurt. Coffee, tea, and milk.

We ate our fill, listening as Farmer assigned jobs to his men, our men volunteering for different chores.

Ava and Ghost sat off to the side, their heads bent together as they ate, no doubt planning what today would bring. I'd heard a whisper Farmer was lending them a vehicle. Ghost had decided not to ride and would be leaving his patch here. I had a suspicion he wanted to go in undercover, ensuring there would be no blowback on the club if shit went south.

"Is it safe for him to go in unidentified?" I asked Wrath. I took a bite of my bread, savouring my first taste.

"Not safe, necessarily." He paused, taking a sip of his coffee. "It makes sense, though. Ghost has often gone undercover. He's been the club's first and last defence when shit goes bad. I have no doubt he'll be fine—the guy has skills that made even the most stoic member of the club nervous."

"And Ava?"

Wrath shrugged. "You'd know better than me."

I took another bite of bread, chewing slowly. "She's fantastic. But that doesn't mean I don't worry about her. Nothing is certain in the after."

Wrath, who was reaching for a second slice of bread, froze. His hand clenched, his expression darkening. Then he relaxed, his face wiped clean as he lifted the bread to his lips.

"W-w-what was that?" I asked, surprise stuttering my words.

"What?"

"That"—I waved my hands at him—"moment you just had. When I said there was no certainty."

He shrugged, chewing.

"Wrath." I narrowed my eyes at him. "What's going on?"

He lifted one shoulder dismissively. "Nothing. You done with those eggs?"

"No." I scooped up a forkful, holding it aloft as I gave him a hard stare. "Why are you being weird?"

"I'm not."

"You are."

"Kate," he huffed out a laugh. "Stop. I'm not being weird. I'm just...." He trailed off.

"Just?" I prompted.

"This seat taken?" Pope dropped into the spare seat beside Wrath, flicking his hair back and shooting me a smile. "You coming hunting with us today, Katie?"

"Don't call her that," Wrath snapped, glaring at Pope.

"What?"

"Her name is Kate. Call her by her fucking name."

I blinked, glancing from Pope to Wrath, a warm, pleasing heat pooling in my belly.

"Geez, sorry." Pope shot me a look. "Are you going hunting with us today, *Kate*?"

I shook my head. "No, I thought I'd check out their crops and greenhouses. They keep mentioning that food stores are low after winter but they're in a good crop yield area. I want to check it out."

Pope nodded, lifting a slice of bread to his mouth. "That's what you did at Uni right?" He tore off a bite, chewing obnoxiously as Audrey settled in the free chair beside him.

I wrinkled my nose. "Yeah, kind of. My speciality was in agriculture. I was studying crop stress tolerance and yield. It wasn't glamourous like some of my peers who were working on saving endangered plants, but I was hoping it would have made a difference to food security as the impacts of climate change became more obvious."

"And now?" Wrath asked.

I shrugged. "With less people and barely any industrial-level production, the world is healing. It won't completely reverse the impact to date, but it'll help." I quirked a smile. "On the upside, I completed two semesters in a lab specialising in medicinal uses for plants. It's come in handy."

"'I'll say." Audrey lifted her mug in my direction. "Kate managed to track down a willow tree. Life. Saver."

"A willow tree?" Pope asked.

"Its bark can be used for pain relief. Like aspirin. In moderation, it's great for small aches and pain."

"Well shit." Pope echoed Audrey's toast, raising his mug to me. "Kudos to you, Mistress Plant. Feel free to inspect every hardwood and mushroom we find. "

I chuckled, accepting the toast with a click of my mug against his.

Wrath stood, reaching for my empty plate. "We should get moving," he told Pope.

Pope shoved the remaining crust in his mouth, dusted off his hands then stood nodding, mouth full.

"Audrey, did you want to help me?" I asked.

She shook her head. "Nah, I'll do laundry. You know I'm likely to kill a plant by just looking at it."

It was true, Audrey may have a brain the size of the moon, but the woman had no skills at growing things.

I left Pope and Audrey arguing over who was more important in the after—a hunter, a forager, a grower, or a creator—and followed Wrath into the kitchen.

"What?" he asked, placing our plates in the sink, water sloshing as he began to clean them.

"You wanna tell me what's going on in your mind?" I asked, leaning a hip against the countertop, arms crossed, eyebrow cocked in question.

"Kate...," he huffed out a laugh. "I'm being a twat."

"Yeah, you are." I laid a hand on his bicep. "Why?"

He cleaned the crockery, his face a war of emotions. Finally, he stepped back, reaching for a towel to dry his hands.

"Life in the after... it's not like the before. I don't have jack-shit to offer you. Not protection, not a place to live, nothing. In the before I had cash. A house. A living. You wanted to travel and I could've made it happen." He shrugged, tossing the towel away. "Now it's just me and a bike. Beyond the club,

I don't got anything to offer you."

"Wrath, don't you realise you're enough?" I gestured around us. "The world's ended and yet we're here. We're full of good food, we've had a good sleep under a safe roof, and today we'll be doing meaningful work. I don't need more than that."

"What about someone to love you?" He stepped toward me, crowding me back towards the counter behind me.

My hands came up, resting against his chest, feeling the warmth of him under my palms. "Maybe…."

"Maybe?" he asked, nuzzling against my neck, his lips grazing the sensitive skin. "What if I said I needed you more than air?"

"That's not love."

"It's not?"

"No, it's obsession."

"Mm." He kissed my shoulder. "Which would you prefer?"

"Love." I tilted my head back, granting him better access. "Obsession is consuming, containing, constraining. It doesn't allow for growth. Love follows you through all seasons of your life. Love is a journey; obsession is a cell."

He pulled back a fraction. "I love you, Kate."

I cupped his face, meeting his gaze. "And I love you, Wrath."

"Kiss me."

Our lips met, our tongues tangling as our hands roamed each other's body, brushing and igniting every nerve ending.

"Hey, Kate are you in—oh! Sorry!"

Wrath pulled back, resting his forehead against mine. "I suspect Audrey won't keep this a secret."

I chuckled. "Probably not."

We stayed like that for a long moment, just basking in each other.

"What's your plan for the day?" he asked.

"Planting, black room, finding a good place for Audrey's equipment." I shrugged. "You know, normal after stuff."

He grinned. "I'll see you after the hunt then."

I kissed him quickly, slipping out from under his arm, calling over my shoulder as I walked away from him, "For luck!"

He stepped quickly, capturing my hand and spinning me back around, kissing me with a breathtaking passion.

"*That's* for luck."

He let me go, walking out of the kitchen with a parting smile.

I leaned back against the counter, the fingers of one hand pressing against my lips.

Oh yeah, I was a very lucky girl.

Chapter Sixteen

Kate

"And you're sure you have everything?" Lottie asked Ava for the tenth time.

"Yes, for the millionth time." Ava cupped Lottie's face pressing her forehead to her sister's. "I'll be back. Afghanistan, Iraq, that time in the Congo—I came back, didn't I?"

Lottie nodded, but I could see her shoulders tremble.

"Don't worry. These kids have got nothing on me."

They embraced, holding tight to each other and for just a fraction longer than someone completely confident of their return would.

Audrey shook her head. "I'm out. Ava, good luck, don't get killed or I'll find a way to clone you and kill you again."

Ava broke away from Lottie, tossing a grin at Audrey. "I don't doubt it." She came over, giving Audrey a quick, one-armed hug. "Don't run into any trouble while I'm gone. And be nice to Pope. He can't help being a doofus."

"No promises."

Jo stepped forward, arms crossed, scowl in place. "Still don't agree with this, but I get it. Just be careful."

"Always."

They clasped forearms; one alpha woman badass to another then both looked away. Ellie stepped into the awkward void.

"There's enough fuel in the SUV to get you there and back, but I've added more in the secret compartment. If you run into trouble, don't be a hero. Runner says Ghost is a good guy to have in an emergency, don't dismiss him because he's a little weird."

Ava rolled her eyes. "A good soldier doesn't reject the resources at her disposal. Even if the resource is a guy who annoys me."

They hugged then Ava turned to me. "You good, Kate?"

I nodded. "You'll bring them home if they're there."

Her lips curved up into a stunning smile. "Ah, my sweet padawan. Your confidence in me brightens my day."

We both chuckled as I wrapped arms around her, giving her a quick squeeze. "Be safe."

"You too."

She stepped back, picked up her backpack then gave us all a jaunty salute. "See you in a few weeks. Make sure that Cunnamulla crew have a cold beer waiting for me."

She headed out, not once looking back as she climbed into the SUV and Ghost started it. The gate slowly swung open and out they drove, bumping down the gravel drive and disappearing into the dense scrub at the base of the hill.

We scattered like lost little ducklings after that. Each of us feeling the loss of Ava keenly.

I found my way to the greenhouses, finding reassurance in the feel of the dirt against my skin.

"Hello," I said, bringing a small clump to my nose and rubbing it between my fingertips, releasing the rich scent of damp earth.

"What secrets would you like to share with me?"

The earth, of course, didn't answer. But the thick, sticky dirt on my fingertips gave me a little indication as to some issues the plants might be facing.

There were four greenhouses in all, each long and high. Two were made from clear PVC panels, a third from thick plastic sheeting with shade netting, and the last was made from glass panels that looked as if they had been removed from various houses and welded together in a slap-dash manner in the after.

I ran my hand over the windows, my palm coming away completely soaked.

"Condensation," I muttered, my fingers twitching for a notepad and pen. The glass greenhouse contained several garden beds, each growing a different crop. Wheat, corn, and rice were all planted in long rows, in addition to another bed that looked to hold some seedling vegetables.

The rice was beginning to show signs of yield, while the wheat and corn were in distress.

I pulled one of the wheat grasses free, examining the roots.

"Kate? You in here?" I heard Audrey call from the other side of the greenhouse.

"Yeah, I'm down by the wheat."

She and Mari made their way over, Mari's eyes bloodshot and puffy.

"You okay?" I asked, discarding the plant, and dusting my dirty hands on my thighs.

"Yeah," she sniffed, tears shimmering once again on her lashes. "We just didn't have all the chemicals for the camera to work."

"But that's okay," Audrey immediately reassured her. "Because she's gonna keep my phone and when we get to the

Plantation, we'll have Shield call her."

I tipped my head to one side, giving Mari a small smile. "You okay with that?"

"Yes," she sniffed again. "But it'll still be a month or so before that happens." She rested a hand on her belly. "Hopefully I'll be able to tell him before this little one makes an appearance."

Audrey shifted, nodding at the wheat. "What's the verdict, Dr Plant?"

"It's early but I suspect the greenhouse is too wet. The rice is growing well because it likes damp soil, but the other crops are drowning and the soil is mouldy."

"Mould?" Mari asked, raising a hand to cover her face.

"Only a little bit. And this form isn't particularly dangerous to humans, though you might be better leaving just in case."

She nodded. "I'll see you guys at lunch."

She waddled away while Audrey crouched down, her glasses slipping forward a fraction. "I didn't know dirt could be mouldy."

"Overwatering or, as I suspect in this instance, in areas of high humidity can cause it to grow. Then you have the plant fighting the mould for nutrients."

"There you go," Audrey muttered, using one of my tweezers to poke at the white clump.

"Hey." I snatched it off her, cleaning the instrument and replacing it back in the leather satchel. "T-t-this was a gift. I don't want to lose it."

My words stuttered just a little. My mother had gifted me the expensive equipment our last Christmas together—just a few months before she passed.

Murdered. Your father murdered her.

A chill ran down my spine, my mind conjuring the image of

Gus lying bleeding on the floor, his face twisted in pain and shock.

No regrets.

It was something Ava had told me the first time I'd been forced to kill a man. We'd met him while out scavenging at a local school. He'd forced Ruby to the ground, desperately ripping at her clothing and fighting for her weapons.

Ava had tackled him, shoving him away, giving me the opportunity to shoot. I'd taken him down with one perfect bullet to the head.

"No regrets," Ava had ordered, helping a sobbing Ruby to her feet. "Don't you regret taking down this piece of shit. We all have choices. He could have approached us, asked for help. He could have left us alone. He could have done another million things instead of attacking. It's kill or be killed out here, Kate. We're choosing to live. You're choosing to live."

We hadn't buried him. Hadn't said a word over his body or offered his soul a prayer. We'd stripped him of anything useful then left him lying in the shadow of the abandoned playground.

He had been the first, and while Gus was my most recent kill, he was unlikely to be my last.

"What can I do to help?"

I pointed at the wheat. "Start pulling them out. I'll assess the roots and we'll see what we can save."

We worked quietly together, my mind on the job but also processing Gus' death.

"Are we murderers?" I asked Audrey as she started on the second garden bed.

"Because we're pulling up plants?"

"No," I huffed out a laugh. "Because we've killed people. And bastards, though you could argue they're more animal than human at this point. Are we murderers?"

She rocked back on her heels, brushing at her cheek, leaving a smudge of dirt behind.

"I guess that depends. Murder is the legal term for an unlawful killing. During war, a soldier can't be charged with murder because it's sanctioned. Then you have self-defence clauses when you kill someone during an altercation etcetera." She shrugged. "Way I see it, the rules and definitions for murder went out the window when the world ended. We're operating by our own rules."

I examined the dirt and roots of the plant in my hand, mulling over her words.

"You're saying that we need to operate by our own moral code?"

She shrugged. "Maybe. But then my moral code could be, don't kill anyone who doesn't attack first. While yours might be kill anyone who gives you a strange look. So how do we reconcile those differences?"

"Rules and laws."

"Uh-huh," she grunted, pulling another plant from the soil, laying it gently down. "It's up to you to decide what's right. In these situations." She gestured vaguely towards the main house. "People gather and order will naturally occur because without it we can't progress. Chaos and destruction stand in the way of progress."

"So, you're saying that as long as everyone within your little group has a clear idea of what constitutes right and wrong, we're fine?"

She nodded. "Look at our group. The women, I mean, I'm still working out the men."

I grinned at her frustrated tone.

"We didn't sit down and work out a moral code or a set of rules. It wasn't explicitly stated what right and wrong was. Instead, we worked together, pulling our weight, and feeling each other out. When something went wrong, we may have all had our own individual thoughts about how to react, but we put that aside to consider the common good."

"So, you're saying murder isn't murder at the moment."

"Do you think it is?"

I considered her words as I placed the plant I was working with on the keep pile.

"No. At least, not any of the kills we've had to do."

"Why?"

"Because… I-I-I guess it was justified. We didn't attack first. Like you said, it was all self-defence."

"And Gus?" she asked.

I sighed, feeling the heavy weight on my soul. "Revenge. But also, justice."

"Because he took your mother's life." It wasn't a question.

"Yes. And for the women he sold while club President. If he could do that, if he could kill a woman or draw a gun on his own daughter, could contemplate selling innocent girls, then I think he would do more."

"Justified homicide," Audrey agreed.

We were quiet for a long time. The piece of me that had been twisted, worried that I was losing the good parts of my soul, unknotted. I felt lighter, less burdened by the weight of my actions.

"Anything else you want to talk about?"

I shook my head.

"You sure?" She waggled her eyebrows meaningfully. "Nothing you want to share about a certain someone?"

I pretended to zip my lips.

Audrey flicked a clump of dirt at me. "Spoilsport!"

"Lunch?" I asked, raising to my feet, and groaning as I stretched.

"Sure, but you're paying."

Chapter Seventeen

Kate

After lunch, Audrey decided to check out the compound. She'd decided that one of the towers might make a good point to anchor a giant transmitter, meaning there was a possibility of setting up a backup relay option should any of the transmitter's we'd used fail.

I left her arguing with one of the locals about radius and equipment to return to the quiet of the plants. I'd need to transfer the healthy, or at least recoverable, crop to a better spot. The glass greenhouse would be fine for the rice over the winter periods, but in summer I worried it would be too hot and needed to think about how I could improve the conditions. Alternatively, I could look at suggesting some vegetables and herbs that would thrive in the hot, humid conditions.

The wheat and corn would need to be moved to a better spot within the next twenty-four hours to give them the best opportunity to survive, and I still needed to assess the other three buildings.

I divided my afternoon between accessing the various crops, testing the soil, and trying to figure out where the plants should be transplanted. By the time I called it a day the sun hung low in the sky, and the compound was once again settling in for the night.

"Lord, you look like something the cat dragged in," Lottie laughed, catching sight of me as I trudged across the yard towards the shower block.

I held up my filthy palms, grinning. "You wanna repeat that?"

She squealed, laughing, and ducking away from me.

"How's Zero?"

Her face dropped. "Not good. The wound was showing signs of infection. Farmer doesn't have the kind of antibiotic we need and Butcher isn't convinced we'll find it on a scavenge around here."

"Options?"

"Farmer says there's a hospital out at Lake Cargelligo."

"How far's that?"

"A little over an hour."

"But?" I asked, crossing my arms, and shivering a little in the cool afternoon breeze.

"Town's besieged by bastards. The residents all moved out onto the lake. Farmer says he and his team went a few months back looking for a doctor but the residents refused to leave. They're convinced the bastards will move on." She shook her head. "Farmer lost two men in that raid."

I blew out a breath. "Second option?"

"We try for Cunnamulla."

"But?"

"It's over six hours travel, he's weak, and I just don't know if they'll have what we need either."

"Have you spoken to Wrath? He's the last who's been through Cunnamulla. He might have an idea of their medical facilities."

"Good idea. He's still out on the hunt but I'll ask when he gets in."

I glanced at the sky. "They're still out?"

"Yeah, Farmer said they'll likely stay until a little after dusk to try and get the bigger game."

I nodded, but my gut pinched with worry. "I should get cleaned up."

"Kate?"

I paused. "Yeah?"

"I'm really worried. I... I think he's going to die."

I sucked in a breath. "I thought he was better."

"The infection...." She shook her head, her curls hanging limp. "I'm trying but between the blood loss, the amputation and the infection I just can't see good things. Even in a hospital setting it would be touch and go. The infirmary here is two steps below a field hospital—and there's no way for us to fly him out to a safer place."

I reached out, pulling her close. "You're doing all you can, Lottie. This isn't your fault."

She let out a broken laugh, sniffing back tears. "I know. It's just... hard. I feel responsible for him. For all of you."

"You're also a vet," I reminded her gently. "Butcher's a paramedic. You guys are doing the best you can with what you have."

"I wish I'd gone to medical school."

I gave her a little shake. "What would Ava say?"

She leaned back, a tiny smile pulling at her lips. "If wishes were horses, we'd be standing waist-deep in horse shit."

We both chuckled.

"Let's get you showered, some food and we'll reassess at dinner." I shrugged. "And who knows, maybe the hunting party stumbled across a doctor. Stranger things have happened."

"From your mouth to God's ears."

I scrubbed myself clean, remembering last night's stolen moments with Wrath in this stall, desire sizzling along my nerves, heating my body.

"Kate! Come on!" Audrey knocked on the stall door interrupting my fantasy. "The murder party is back."

"Murder party?" I asked, shutting off the water and reaching for a towel.

"Meat is murder, tasty delicious murder. Now come *on!*"

I dressed, exiting the stall, and following Audrey as I tugged on my jacket.

"Hurry!" Audrey called, practically skipping.

"What's the rush?"

She didn't answer but she didn't need to as we rounded one of the buildings, coming to the middle of the yard.

"W-w-what the h-h-hell is that?" I asked, tripping to a stop in surprise.

"Llamas!" Audrey cried, practically jumping up and down with excitement. "They found llamas and sheep! Sheep, Kate." She grabbed my hands dancing us in a circle. "Sheep and llamas, llamas and sheep. Meat and wool and protection for the lambies!"

I laughed, shaking my head. "You're a nut."

"No, I'm just right."

Wrath came over, his grin way too attractive when there were other people around and I couldn't do more than give him a chaste kiss and hug.

If only you'd been home earlier to join me in the shower.

He smelled of sweat and dirt, of sun and travel. There was a fine layer of grit across his skin, but it suited him.

"You okay?" I asked, letting him pull me into him.

"Now I am." He nuzzled my neck, pressing a kiss to my pulse point. "Should have waited for me. We could have saved water."

I chuckled, closing my eyes as his lips brushed my skin.

"Wrath, there are people around."

"They're watching the llamas, not us."

I gave in, letting him kiss his way up my neck across my cheek and to my mouth. He paused, a mere breath away from my lips.

"Miss me, Sunshine?"

"Always," I whispered, loving how his eyes darkened in response.

"Wrath! We need a hand," Runner called.

"Give me a sec." He captured my mouth in a hot kiss. The chaste kiss I'd envisioned was obliterated as he feasted on my mouth, teasing and stroking, as if he'd been gone for a decade rather than the few hours it had been.

"Wrath!"

He pulled back, shooting me another devilish grin. "Duty calls."

Whistling, he headed back to the mess of people, animals and—strangely—a chicken, wading in with purpose.

I lifted a hand, touching my lips.

Oh, he is trouble.

Chapter Eighteen

Kate

With the arrival of the flock, the barn became a place to house animals rather than humans. The hayloft would do us for tonight, but tomorrow we'd need to reassess our accommodation.

Dinner was postponed while we all pitched in to stable the animals—Lottie assessing each one as they came in.

We finally settled, sharing stew and flatbread while Butcher provided the update on Zero.

"Cunnamulla was hurting last time I passed through," Wrath said, shaking his head. "Unless they've managed to get extra supplies since I left, your best option might be to try for the local hospital."

Farmer shook his head. "I lost men last time. The bastards had completely taken it over."

"But you said they had a doctor?" Butcher pressed.

Farmer nodded slowly. "An older woman, Justine. But she refused to leave the residents. And those sons of bitches weren't prepared to abandon the town."

"When were you last there?" Jo asked, her head tipped slightly to the side.

"About six months."

"Before winter," Audrey muttered. "They might be getting desperate."

"And, no offence, but you need them here." I waved my hand towards the windows. "Your crops are shit. You guys might be good hunters but you don't know how to grow crops. Offer them protection here. Build a community."

Farmer frowned, looking around the table. "Here?"

"Did you offer that to begin with?" Audrey asked.

He shrugged. "I offered to help them, sure."

"That's a no," Pope muttered, absently stirring his stew.

"Look, we had our own shit to deal with. I offered to give them safe passage outta town, they refused. We got what we needed and came back two men short. What else you want me to say?"

Ellie waved a hand dismissively. "That's in the past. What we're talking about is your future, Farmer. If you want to run this as a thriving commune you need to diversify your skillset."

He rolled his eyes. "You think I don't know that?"

"So, you'll offer them safety here? Give them an option to join you?"

He looked at Mari who smiled, her hand resting gently on her belly.

"We don't know these people."

"Every opportunity carries risk."

Farmer blew out a long breath. "I'll think about it."

"But we're going, yeah?" Swift looked around at our group. "We're gonna hit that hospital, see if they got the shit for Zero?"

Runner nodded. "We don't have a choice."

"Butcher, me, and Texas." Wrath declared. "We'll go."

"Excuse me?" I looked at him, my eyebrows raising. "You think three of you will be enough to tackle an entire horde?"

"No, but that's not the plan."

"You wanna enlighten the rest of us?" Texas asked, crossing his arms, and tapping one foot.

"We go in quiet. Fewer people means we can move quicker. We set up a distraction, push the bastards out that direction, away from the hospital. Two of us go in, get what we need, the other stands guard. In and out. Done."

"Uh-huh," Audrey said, her eyes closed. "And how big is the hospital?"

Farmer shrugged. "Don't know. It's a regional hospital. So, like the size of a big clinic."

Audrey opened her eyes just to glare at him. "And that means?"

He shrugged again. "As big as it needs to be."

"Jesus." She threw her arms up. "How am I meant to run numbers when I'm dealing with shit like this." She turned to Wrath. "I'm giving you a thirteen percent chance of success. Your assumption is premised on you being able to control the bastards, and that the townspeople haven't retaken some of their area. You need more people to improve your chances."

She turned, pointing at Farmer. "And you have a thirty-three percent chance of surviving another year. Your chances go down if you keep fucking up your crops and don't get more people in to assist. Fatigue management is gonna be an issue, you'll have kids running around here soon, not to mention scarcity of food will have bastards scratching at your door."

She crossed her arms, giving one final nod. "Questions?"

Wrath leaned over, his breath brushing the shell of my ear. "She's fucking terrifying sometimes."

I turned, my lips brushing his slightly as I grinned. "She's gonna rule this post-apocalyptic world by Christmas."

"No doubt."

He leaned in, kissing me gently before pulling back.

"What was that for?"

He shrugged. "Because I could."

My body tingled, a pleasant warmth pooling in my belly.

"Alright," Pope said, spooning up a scoop of his stew. "So what's the solution to our scenario percentage?"

"Jo and Kate need to go as well, they're the best shots," Audrey said with a nod. "Lottie, Ellie, Runner and Swift need to stay here and make sure they get to the next pitstop if we fail. Ellie's too valuable to lose, and Lottie needs to keep nursing Zero."

"And you and me?" Pope asked, raising an eyebrow.

"As much as I hate looking at your face, I know you have experience with explosives." Audrey clapped her hands together then threw them out wide. "We're the bomb and distraction squad. Our main goal will be to continually stay one step ahead of the bastards while these guys get in and out. And talk with the townies."

"You think we're gonna have time for a little chit-chat?" Pope scoffed.

"We will if we do it right."

"So, it's settled?" Jo asked, looking around the room. "We leave at first light?"

There were nods.

"Let's just hope Zero makes it through the night, poor bastard," Butcher muttered, staring into his mug.

"You finished?" Wrath asked me.

I looked down at my bowl. "Yeah?"

He reached for my hand, hauling me up and leading me from

the room.

"Hey! You forgot to put your bowls away!" Pope yelled after us.

"Take care of it for me, we're busy."

Laughter followed us as Wrath towed me away from our gathering and into the cold night.

"Wrath?"

"What?"

"Where are we going?"

"Somewhere private. I need to taste you."

"Oh… in that case, lead on."

Chapter Nineteen

Wrath

I took Kate to the escape tower, helping her climb to the top.

"You know," she huffed, sprawling out on the wooden floor of the platform. "I wasn't expecting my fitness to be judged tonight."

I grinned, crawling up beside her pulling the trap door shut behind us. "Catch your breath then come have a look."

While she panted, sucking in air, I spread a blanket and pulled two bottles of beer from my backpack, the moon lighting the small area.

The escape tower sat at the highest part of the yard. The platform had enough room for most of the occupants of the compound, though they wouldn't be here for long. The platform was set up with kill holes, extra ammunition and bug-out bags. A zip line ran from the top of the platform disappearing down the hill and into the bush that surrounded the bottom of the property. Hidden in amongst the brush were escape vehicles and hidey-holes, ready for a worst-case scenario.

"This is incredible," Kate whispered, running her hand over

the harnesses hung neatly on the wall. "And terrifying."

"In the after nothing is guaranteed. The compound is secure, but if a militia group with a tank arrived, they wouldn't stand for long." I wrapped my arms around her, breathing in her clean, fresh scent. "We can't predict our tomorrows, Kate. We can only live in the now."

She chuckled, leaning back against me, tilting her head until her gaze met mine. "So, you admit I'm right then?"

I kissed her, tasting that chuckle on her tongue, loving the feel of her in my arms. "Always," I whispered, pressing another kiss to her lips. "But it doesn't mean I'm not terrified that you've chosen me."

Kate twisted, her hands coming up to cup my cheeks, searching my face. "I'd choose you every time, Wrath."

I swallowed. "You didn't always feel like that."

She raised an eyebrow in question.

"Blake Jimson."

She coughed, spluttering as I dredged up that fucktard.

"Oh God." She leaned into me, her arms linking around my neck. "If I'd had even an inkling that you might like me, I'd have never even looked his way." She shook her head, her stutter coming back for a moment. "B-b-b-biggest regret e-e-ever."

I grappled with myself for a moment, contemplating whether to tell her my darkest secret.

"Kate?"

"Mm?"

"I beat the shit out of him."

She blinked, staring up at me, her eyes wide, her mind rapidly connecting the dots. "Oh my God. Wrath… that extra year you spent as a prospect…you said you'd gone against orders."

I shrugged, uncomfortable but needing her to know how

much I'd wanted her since the beginning. "He hurt you. All those fuckers at that shitty school did. So, I just did what I needed to."

"But you went against Gus. For me."

"Ain't that big a deal, Kate. You deserved someone looking out for you."

She dropped to her knees, her fingers fumbling with my belt.

"Hey." I grabbed her hands, stilling her movement. "What're you doing?"

"You're gonna let me give you a blowjob right now, Wrath," she said, glaring at me. "And you're gonna fucking like it."

I laughed, still holding her hands. "Sunshine, I don't need a blow job. I didn't tell you that to get anything from you. I don't want a pity blowjob."

"It's not a pity blowjob!"

"Fine, a thankyou blowjob then."

"It's not either of those!" She shook at my hands but I held her firm. "I'm wetter than sin right now. You defended me, Wrath. And that's hot as fuck."

I hesitated, seeing the heat in her gaze, her beautiful eyes flashing.

"Just so we're clear, you know you don't have to do this right? I brought you up here so I could eat you out, not get sucked off."

She nodded, licking her lips.

"Then have at it." I released her hands, chuckling as she eagerly fumbled with my belt and fly. My amusement fled as Kate wrapped her fingers around my cock, pulling me free. My dick was hard, hot, and aching. Had been since before I'd led her from the dining room. Just being near her was intoxicating. She fucked with my senses, I wanted to rub myself over her, come on her, mark her; the possessive part of me roaring a demand.

Kate's greedy mouth pressed hot kisses up and down my length, her tongue teasing and tasting as her fingers gripped the base of my cock, holding me steady.

"Fuck," I groaned, my head dropping back, hand coming up to lightly fist her hair. "You're amazing."

She chuckled, the heat of her breath adding to the moment. "Brace, Wrath."

I looked down, nearly losing my control as she wrapped her lips around my cock, pressing forward until she had me seated deep in her throat.

"Jesus, fuck, Christ, motherfucker," the curses spilled from my lips, dotted with praise for her as she began to rock, her mouth gliding up and down my length, her glorious tongue playing at the sensitive underside of my crown before returning once more to suck me down.

"Christ, Kate. You're sinfully good at this, Sunshine. Gonna come soon."

She made a sound in the back of her throat, something eager and encouraging, her movements enthusiastic if clumsy. It was messy, wet, hot and everything I'd ever dreamed of.

"Kate, wait," I panted, trying to hold her steady, to stop her movement. But she ignored me, doubling down, her mouth hot and fucking amazing as she worked me over.

"Fuck," I groaned, giving in. "Gonna come."

She pulled back just as I came, cum decorating the swell of her tits and the top of her shirt as she panted, her eyes wide and gloriously heated as I pulsed, marking her delicate skin.

I dropped to my knees, wrapping arms around her as I lowered her to the floor. My cock needed a minute but hot desire and desperate need rode me hard.

"Wrath, what—" Kate bit off, her body arching as my hand slipped into her jeans, finding her wet little pussy.

"You're gonna come just for me, aren't you, Sunshine? Gonna ride my fingers until you feel as good as you just made me."

She whimpered, the sound desperate, her hips flexing.

I kissed her as her body stiffened, my fingers stroking her, pressing until she ripped her mouth away, her head bowing as she came on a strangled scream.

My cock reared up, suddenly keen for round two.

With the scent of Kate on the air, I stripped her clothes from her body, then pulled my own free. Her hands branded me, her gaze hungry as she stroked and touched, her mouth just as eager.

I returned the favour, laving her breasts, licking and sucking her large nipples, alternating until she protested, her hips now in constant motion.

"Now," she pleaded, her hands trying to pull me over her. "Please, Wrath, now."

I gave her what she wanted, rolling us onto the blanket, my body covering hers.

"Ready?"

Kate nodded, her smile wide and a little nervous.

"I got you, Sunshine, promise."

"I know, love you."

"Love you too, now let me concentrate." I kissed her smiling mouth. "Gotta make sure I get this right."

She cupped my head, kissing me, our tongues dancing as I fed her my cock, her tight pussy gripping me like a vice.

Mine. Mine. MINE.

"Jesus," I breathed against her lips, sweat pouring down my

body as I struggled for control. "Fuck, Kate. So, fucking tight."

She panted under me, her body shifting. "Are you—"

I cut her question off by surging forward. She sucked in a breath, flinching.

"Sorry, oh God, I'm so sorry, Sunshine." I peppered kisses over her skin, hating that where I felt heaven, she only felt pain.

I let her adjust, in no rush to have this moment finished.

"I-I-I think you can k-k-keep going," Kate whispered, her voice stuttering.

"Sure?"

She nodded, her hips beginning to move restlessly. "Oh yes."

I shifted a little, creating space between us, pushing up slightly to better reach her breasts.

"W-w-what are you doing?"

"If I have to tell you, I mustn't be doing it right." I shot her a grin, lowering my head until I could taste her creamy breast.

She made a hot little sound, her eyes closing as I lapped her nipple, sucking her into my mouth, my tongue teasing.

"Good?" I asked, shifting to her other breast.

Kate nodded, seemingly incapable of words.

I shifted, stroking my cock into her, watching carefully for her reaction. Her eyes flew open, her mouth forming an O-shape.

"Wrath!"

I grinned, gently dragging my teeth over her breast, my hips finding a lazy rhythm. "Mm?"

"Wrath, oh Wrath."

Fuck I like that.

I drove harder, pressing kisses up her collarbone, across her throat, sucking her earlobe and nipping at her chin. Kate clenched in response, her fingernails scratching across my back, marking me. I found her lips, kissing her hard and hot, our mouths fucking in time with our bodies.

I tasted the desperate need for release on her tongue.

"I got you, Kate. You're safe."

With another thrust, I slid home, bottoming out. Kate arched, her restraint gone as she came, her teeth biting into my shoulder, her pussy milking my cock.

Don't come, don't come, don't—

"Wrath!"

I lost all control, meeting her need with a hot fucking. I thrust into her, marking her, losing my mind with the knowledge I was her first, her only.

Mine. Mine. Mine.

I collapsed on her, sweat cooling on our skin.

I pressed lazy kisses to her skin, my body spent but my soul demanding I keep going. I needed to fuck her, love her, mark her until we were inexplicably entwined.

Forever.

Obsession is consuming, containing, constraining. It doesn't allow for growth. Love follows you through all seasons of your life. Love is a journey; obsession is a cell.

Kate's words from earlier rattled through my brain, cooling my blood slightly.

I didn't want to control her. I wanted her to choose to be with me. I loved her.

This is love.

I lifted, looking down into her sleepy face.

"I love you, Sunshine. So, fucking much."

Her grin was perfection.

"If we can go another round before bed, I might love you just as much."

I threw back my head and laughed.

Chapter Twenty

Wrath

We left the next morning, Farmer loaning us trucks and an SUV. His men acted as if they were sending us to our death, stony-faced and dead-eyed.

Fuckers.

Runner clasped my hand, pulling me in. "No unnecessary risks. If you get there and it's too much, bail."

I nodded, squeezing his hand. "No risks."

We left, bumping along the dirt road down into the valley and out to the main road, hitting what felt like every pothole and divot along the way. I caught Kate wincing.

"You okay?"

She huffed out an embarrassed laugh. "Yeah just... tight."

"Ah..." Call me a dick, but I couldn't quite help feeling satisfied and a little arrogant.

Audrey leaned forward from her position on the back seat, placing a hand on Kate's neck. "You okay? Need me to rub anything? Maybe you shouldn't have spent all day yesterday digging."

Kate's face flamed, her head dropping forward to hide her

mortified expression. "I-I-I-I'll be f-f-fine. Just n-n-n-need to st-st-stretch my legs."

Audrey nodded, giving Kate's neck a little squeeze then sitting back. Ahead of us, Pope rode point on his bike, Texas and Jo were just behind in a second SUV, with Butcher bringing up the rear in a Jeep.

I caught sight of something out of the corner of my eye.

"Is that—"

I nodded, my lips pressing into a thin line. "Bastards."

The horde had gathered near a small creek bed, some crouched, others shifting restlessly. They were far enough away not to be of concern, just caution.

"I just don't understand. Where did they come from? The virus didn't do this. The virus just killed people."

I shrugged, picking up speed as we traded dirt and gravel roads for worn bitumen.

The rest of the drive was uneventful, only needing to slow for the occasional meandering cow or mob of kangaroos.

Pope lifted a hand, waving us over to the side of the road as we hit the outskirts of town.

I unbuckled, pointing at Audrey and Kate. "Stay here. Anything happens, get the fuck out of here. Got me?"

Audrey nodded but Kate bit her lip, her expression conflicted.

"I mean it, Sunshine. I can take care of myself but I can't do that worrying about you."

She nodded, reaching out to catch my hand and give it a squeeze before I exited the car. I met the men at Pope's bike.

"Seems quiet," Butcher remarked as he scanned the landscape around us. Beside him, Texas palmed his gun, doing the same.

"Thoughts?" Pope asked, deferring to me.

I rubbed my chin, running scenarios in my mind.

"Pope, get Audrey for me."

He sighed, then headed to the truck, calling, "Oh love of my heart, come out and meet thy hero."

"What are you thinking?" Butcher asked, his voice low.

"Pope's a joker but he's deadly in a jam. I'm thinking he and I go in on foot, we check the place out then circle back with a plan."

"And Audrey?"

I blew out a sigh. "She's good. Her brain is like a computer—she processes the options and risks faster than the rest of us. We'll take her with us, she can help build the plan."

Texas shook his head, his mouth thinning. "Jo's not gonna like that."

"She might not, but it's the best option we have."

We made space for Audrey and Pope, the former crossing her arms as she glared at each of us. "Why do I get the feeling I'm not gonna like this little powwow?"

"We need you to come on a recon mission. I need your brain to help figure out our plan of attack."

Audrey shuddered, her shoulders slumping slightly. "Thank God for Ava."

"Ava?"

Audrey nodded. "Ava's first rule, cardio saves lives." She shuddered again. "Running from zombies is an unappealing thought but the second option of becoming a member of the walking dead is worse."

I sighed, not even bothering to correct her.

Audrey squatted down then stood up, jumping a few times, shaking out her arms.

"What are you doing?" Pope asked, eyebrow raised.

"Stretching. Warming up. Gotta be limber before taking on a sprint." She stopped for a moment nodding at me and shoving her glasses up her nose. "You do the same, right?"

"Yeah, as the occasion calls for it."

She pulled one arm across her chest, stretching her shoulders with a satisfied smile. "I'm no zombie snack today."

Pope rolled his eyes, turning away from Audrey. "Plan?"

"You, me and Audrey go in, survey the place." I pointed at the water tower which stood slightly taller than the rest of the buildings in town. "If we can get there and make the roof, it'll give us a decent vantage point."

"And the townspeople?" Audrey asked, now holding one foot to her butt, her free hand tightly gripping Texas' bicep for balance as she stretched her glutes.

"We'll make that decision once we see what we're up against."

Texas distributed weapons, hesitating before handing over a small pistol to Audrey. "You're sure you know how to use this?"

She rolled her eyes. "Puh-lease. Ava was training us on machine guns. This peashooter is hardly a concern." She checked the safety, then tucked it into her pants pocket.

"Right, we moving now or…?"

I glanced at the other men, all of whom were looking various levels of amused.

"Give me five then we move out."

I headed to Kate, finding her wide-eyed in the driver's seat of the first SUV. She wound the window down, waiting for me to reach her.

"We're heading off, Sunshine. Audrey's coming with us."

She looked at the town in the distance, scrutinising the landmarks before nodding. "You'll want her to map the grounds and work out the best options for us."

I grinned, loving how her mind worked. "Yep."

She reached out, cupping my face, her thumb grazing my cheek. "Be careful. I love you."

My reply sounded rough. "Love you too. Remember, no stupid risks."

She grinned. "Same to you."

I leaned in claiming her with a hot, demanding kiss, imprinting her with my taste. I pulled back, sucking in a deep breath, memorising her face one last time before turning to the town, my focus shifting to the job at hand.

Get in, get out, get back to Kate.

I cleared my throat, calling, "Let's go."

Chapter Twenty-One

Wrath

We crept through the abandoned township, Pope at the rear, Audrey in the middle and me taking point. Red dirt covered the streets, the light wind whipping up the dust.

"Feels like a cheap western," Audrey muttered behind me.

A growl sounded to the left of us. I whipped around, gun pointed towards the sound.

A small dog, mangy and starving, crawled out of a hole in the building. He growled again; his hackles raised as he stared us down.

"Hey, pup." Pope shifted, stepping away from where he'd protectively pressed Audrey into the brick of the building behind us. "We're not bastards. See?" He flexed his hands, opening and closing them in a way no bastard could. "Only good old-fashioned humans here."

The dog's hackles lowered, his head tilting to one side as he watched us.

"Come on," I muttered, looking around the side of the building. "Coast is clear. Let's go."

We crept along, the dog trailing. Apart from dirt and some

plant matter that had accrued in gutters, the town was in surprisingly good shape. We passed stores with canned goods still on shelves, and clothing stores with shirts hanging limply in abandoned windows.

"Where are all the people?" Audrey asked when we paused on the main street. "And the zombies?"

Pope circled in, the dog following behind him. "I don't like this. Something feels off."

I nodded, the hairs rising on the back of my neck.

"Keep moving."

We made it to the water tower, finding the stairs and beginning the climb to the top. Pope took up residence on the stairs as Audrey and I made it to the platform, walking around the tower to survey the town.

"No bastards," Audrey said, lifting a hand to shade her face. "Have they moved on?"

I shook my head, palming the gun in my hand. "Somethings wrong."

"Everything looks fine."

I nodded, shaking off my unease. "Okay, map it out for me."

She considered the lay of the land, her eyes scanning the town. "Hospital is off to the side, shouldn't be too hard. We should try and bring some supplies back with us, and reach out to that doctor. I say we split up. Butcher, you and Kate hit the hospital. Texas and Jo can raid, Pope and I can search for survivors."

I raised an eyebrow.

"Just because he drives me to drink doesn't mean I don't see his potential. He's charming. I'm analytical. Between the two of us, we've got a better chance of convincing them of leaving than—"

A terrible howl interrupted her. We both jumped, immediately staring down over the safety rail to see the dog, howling like the devil was on his tail, taking off towards the water.

"What the fuck!" Movement to the left caught my eye.

"Fuck! We gotta go!"

I grabbed her hand, tugging her along behind me as we ran down the stairs, Pope standing at the bottom, yelling at us to run.

"Water or back?" Pope yelled.

"Water!" Audrey barked, bolting down the walk, following the footprints left by the dog. "Hurry!"

We chased her, the horde now crashing through the streets behind us, their grunts, and growls loud in the quiet afternoon.

"Faster," Pope yelled, grabbing Audrey's arm, pulling her along. "They're gaining!"

I chanced a glance, catching sight of the leaders of the pack—a woman in torn fatigues, and a man who looked like a local farmer, his jeans ripped to shit, the remains of a plaid shirt hanging off one arm. Both were frothing at the mouth, their skin sagging, bodies thin.

"The dog!"

I whipped my head around, managing to catch sight of the dog as it disappeared down a small deck and took a flying leap into the lake.

"This better work!" Pope bellowed sprinting to the end and leaping off, Audrey's hand clasped firmly in his as they hit the water, disappearing below.

I took a flying leap, following them into the lake, hitting with a crash, water enveloping me.

The image of Kate under me, her beautiful smile wide and slightly dazed as I came in her once more was my final thought as I sank into the murky water.

Chapter Twenty-Two

Wrath

I kicked to the surface, my lungs burning for air, bastards falling into the water and thrashing around me as they drowned.

That was the thing about being a mindless beast, you didn't have the sense to climb or swim.

I kicked forward, stroking out towards Pope and Audrey who were headed to a floating platform in the middle of the lake.

"Is that the dog?" I asked, falling in beside them as we all breaststroked towards the platform.

"Yep."

As we swam closer, I could see the platform was a makeshift floating jetty, coupled together in a hodgepodge of barrels and planks. Rough tents made from tarps and blankets, and wooden containers holding wilting plants lined the sides.

I slowed, Pope doing the same. Audrey kept stroking for the platform but Pope reached out, capturing her foot, and pulling her back.

"What?" she asked, treading water. "It's right there."

"Think, Brainy Girl," Pope said, nodding at the platform.

She considered it, her lips pressing together.

"Where are the people?"

Good question.

"I don't like this." Pope twisted looking back at the jetty where those bastards who hadn't fallen into the lake continued to pace, growling and spitting.

"Well, just to say, I'm happier to take my chances with ghost island than zombie beach." Audrey pushed forward, the water sloshing around us. "Come on."

"Let Pope go first," I told her, following.

"That's right, watch me put my attractive arse on the line for you miscreants." Pope reached for the jetty, he pulled a knife from his belt, gripping it between his teeth and climbing up.

"Miscreants? Wow, fancy word for a man who can barely cogitate."

Pope stood, looking around. "Clear. Like, frighteningly clear."

I tossed my wet pistol onto the jetty then helped Audrey up, following her a moment later. The deck looked like a ghost town, the tents flapping uselessly in the slight breeze.

"Audrey, get your knife out."

She pulled it from her boot, holding it awkwardly.

It'll have to do.

"Stay close to Pope. Pope…." I gave him a look. He nodded; any amusement wiped from his face.

"Can you smell that?" Audrey whispered as Pope peeled back the flaps of one tent.

"Jesus." He let the cloth drop but not before I caught a glimpse of a decaying body.

"Are they… dead?" Audrey asked, gripping the handle of her

knife.

I pressed a hand to her back. "Let's keep moving."

The platform was bigger than it first looked, stretching out the size of a half football field. The platform held nothing but rotting bodies and abandoned tents.

"I… I can't," Audrey whispered, her voice breaking when we stumbled across a family.

Pope pulled her into him, shielding her face, his arms wrapped tight around her.

"Wrath, we need to go. This is…"

"A slaughter."

And not by the bastards. This was a cold-blooded execution of people trying to live their life in the after.

"Best way off?" Pope asked.

I looked around, spotting the dog following us at a distance.

"Let's head for the other end of the lake. We can loop past the hospital. It'll be a longer journey but at least we know there's nothing for us here."

Pope turned Audrey slightly. When she went to lift her head and shift away from him, he caught her face turning it into him.

"Don't look, just let me guide you."

I followed gut rolling, rage ripping my insides apart.

Whoever had done this would pay.

Back in the water, we swam to shore, stepping out of the lake and into an abandoned street. The dog trailed us once more, shaking off the water and following quietly as we ran through the streets, ducking and diving around corners until we found the hospital.

"Hold, movement," Pope whispered, capturing Audrey's hand. "Second door."

A man holding a cigarette puffed it slowly, a gun slung around his shoulder. He watched the street with the idle comfort of someone who didn't expect an ambush.

"Friend or foe?" I asked, watching him flick the cigarette to the ground then disappear back inside.

"Foe. Third window on the right."

I looked up, following Pope's direction. A woman stood in the window, her gaze locked on us. She wore a bloodied shirt, her hair fell limp about her, her skin bruised. Raising a hand to the window she mouthed one word.

Help.

"Fuck." Audrey shifted, immediately alert. "How many?"

The woman turned away presenting us her back. She stood frozen for a moment then left, the curtain falling back into place.

"Let's regroup with the others," I said, my voice low as I watched the street, checking for danger. "We've been gone long enough."

The dog followed as we ran back to our team, bitter rage burning a hole in my gut.

God have mercy on them because I certainly wouldn't.

Chapter Twenty-Three

Kate

I drummed my fingers across the steering wheel, nervously watching the township.

"They've been gone a while," I muttered.

"Progress!" Jo tapped her watch, shooting me a grin. "You went a full minute this time."

"Shut up."

Jo pretended to flick her short brunette hair back, the sassy action reminiscent of reality TV stars from the before. "Yes, mistress."

I breathed out, trying not to fret.

"Yo." Texas appeared at Jo's window, giving it a tap. "I got news."

Jo rolled it down and he leaned into the cab snatching one of the water bottles from the dash.

"Just help yourself there, champ."

"Don't mind if I do." Texas winked at her over the bottle, his throat moving as he swallowed.

Jo rolled her eyes, but I caught the slight flush heating her cheeks.

"You said you had news?"

He lowered the bottle, wiping his mouth with his forearm. "There's a horde down the road. Shackled in a pen. Looks like the local showgrounds got turned into a meat yard."

I wrinkled my nose. "Meat yard?"

"Or holding pen. Zoo? Whatever word you wanna use for it, someone managed to entice a shit ton of those fuckers and lock 'em up."

"But they didn't kill them?" Jo asked.

"Nope." Texas raised his water bottle, pausing at his lips. "Makes me wonder if the horde includes some locals. People get right sentimental some times."

Something shifted at the corner of my eye, catching my attention. "Is that a dust storm?"

Texas and Jo looked out towards the town, a dust cloud rising from the centre.

Jo pointed at the trees in the distance. "No breeze."

Something insidious and cold slithered down my spine, curling in my gut. "It's a horde."

"Surely not…." Texas trailed off as we watched the dust cloud move across the town, heading toward the water.

"I don't like this," Jo whispered. "This feels off."

"It's gotta be a horde. Shit." I death-gripped the steering wheel, my fingers itching to start the truck and search for Wrath. "Do you think they're in trouble?"

"Even if they are, we can't do anything." Jo reached out, squeezing my arm. "They'll be okay, Kate. Have faith."

I swallowed, nodding.

Texas reached out, grabbing another water from the carton resting on the dash. "Gonna head back to the car. Butcher will be fretting. Stay in here, don't do anything stupid."

He stepped back, waiting until Jo rewound the window, sealing us in before heading back to his car.

"It really is okay, Kate. Between Pope, Wrath and Audrey they'll work it out."

I nodded, trying to will myself to feel the same confidence she felt. Silence fell in the cab, Jo and I watching as the dust cloud dissipated but our crew didn't appear.

Come on. Come back to me Wrath.

The day stretched, the sun sinking low in the sky. Jo sucked in a breath, both of us freezing as a bastard stumbled down the street, spitting and growling, he ignored our parked vehicles, disappearing down another street.

"They're weird-looking," Jo finally said, sinking back in her seat. "Kind of reminds me of kids playing dinosaur."

"Really?"

Jo nodded, lifting her hands, and curling them into claws. "Like this." She pawed at the air, making a growling sound that I assumed was meant to be a roar but sounded more like a Wookie. A reluctant smile tugged at my lips.

She sobered, dropping her hands, giving me a look. "Do you love him?"

I swallowed, looking back out at the deserted town. "Y-yeah."

She sighed, her hands rubbing at her face. "We're dropping like goddamned flies."

"Excuse me?"

"First Ellie, now you. Who's next? Ava?"

I barked out a laugh. "Ava would cut a guy's dick off before he could even think about it."

We both sniggered.

"I miss her," I admitted. "I miss them all."

"She's only been gone a day. And we've been gone less than

a week."

I noticed that she skirted over Jules and Lilith.

"Don't you miss your sisters?"

Jo rubbed a hand over her face, shaking her head. "Sure, but they'll be fine without me. We're doing important work here."

Movement caught my eye. "It's Wrath!"

I scrambled for the door handle, throwing the door open and running down the dirt road to wrap myself around him.

"Sunshine." He gripped me tight, his mouth finding mine. Hot, wet, and demanding; I gave in, sinking into him, letting him brand me.

"Kate! We got chased by zombies! We had to dive into the lake to escape them!"

Audrey's chatter broke through, Wrath pulling back slightly to look at me.

"You're okay?" I whispered, ignoring Audrey.

"Now I am." He offered me a crooked smile.

I melted, sinking against him. "Love you."

"Love you too, Sunshine." He pulled me in, pressing a kiss to my forehead before shifting us around to follow Audrey. "Come on, we need to do a debrief."

We headed for the SUVs gathering around the front of the first vehicle.

"The citizens are gone." Pope started, rubbing a hand across his chest. "Massacre. Not sure who but there're people at the hospital who might know."

"Did you talk to them?" Butcher asked. "Are they open to trade?"

Audrey shook her head, her arms wrapped tight around her. "We saw one guy with a gun, and a woman in a window. The woman looked shit scared, and asked for help."

"We're gonna have to go in," Wrath said, pulling me into his side. "Whatever happened on the floating city isn't over."

"And the bastards?" Jo asked.

"There's a horde, but they're hanging out down by the lake."

Audrey hit Pope, rolling her eyes. "What he fails to tell you is that we barely escaped them."

I looked up at Wrath, seeking confirmation. He shrugged, not correcting her description.

What the fuck?

Texas explained about the penned bastards down at the showground then looked to Wrath. "Plan?"

"Audrey?" Wrath asked, deferring to her.

She pressed her lips together, her eyes closing for a moment.

"Nightfall. We need to go in quiet. Jo and Kate lying in wait as snipers. Wrath, Pope and Butcher laying down cover. Texas, you'll organise the distraction—preferably not in the form of the showground but do what you gotta."

"And you?" Pope asked.

"I'll be bait."

"What?!"

"Hell no!"

"Over my dead body!"

Audrey waved away the group's protests. "Let me explain."

Calmly she laid out the plan, mapping contingencies and options.

"Thoughts?" she asked, looking around the group.

Butcher blew out a breath, running a hand through his hair, leaving a mess in his wake. "It's good. Real fucking good."

"Agreed." Wrath nodded. "Any objections?"

Everyone shook their heads.

"Then let's go find a place to rest. Tonight's gonna be here soon enough."

Chapter Twenty-Four

Wrath

The afternoon shadows grew long, the day bleeding into night. A sunset of fire painted the spring sky brilliant reds, oranges, and purples. This land was big sky country, and while I didn't put much stock in signs, it felt as if the sky were asking us to burn the fuckers to the ground.

Or maybe that was just me, looking for signs that would grant permission for me to unleash the toxic bitter rage in my gut.

Kate handed me a protein bar, making a face as she bit into her own.

"Not good?" I asked, watching her with a grin.

"Look, it's not bad it's just…." She trailed off, munching the tough slice.

"Fucking terrible," I finished for her, chewing off one end. "They always are."

We ate in silence, our legs pressed together as we watched the sunset.

"Audrey's adopted the dog." Kate folded the plastic in her hand, tucking it into the junk bag we'd brought with us. We'd get rid of it when we stumbled across the next dump.

Hey, the world may have ended but that didn't mean we couldn't be tidy.

"The pup saved our lives," I said, grimacing as I took another bite of the shitty bar.

"And for that, he'll be getting roo meat when we return." Her lips quirked. "I like him, but I'm not putting him in the car with us. He smells horrible."

I laughed, twisting to pull her into me and snuggle against her neck. "Mm, you, however, smell amazing."

She giggled, twisting to get away. "And you smell like dirty swamp water."

I let her go, sitting back and resigning myself to the last bites of our dinner. "You remember the plan?"

She rolled her eyes but nodded. "Jo and I take sniper points. You, Butcher, Audrey, and Pope go in. Texas does perimeter and bastards."

I nodded, trying to get a handle on my rage. "If you get made, or someone finds you, shoot until you can get to safety. Don't bullshit me, Kate. I need you to promise that you'll shoot first and ask later."

She nodded, all gentle amusement wiped from her expression. "I promise. No chances. That goes for y-y-you too."

The slight waiver of her voice, the slip of her stutter, revealed just how stressed and anxious she was about tonight. I pulled her into my chest, wrapping my arms tight around her, the sun finally disappearing over the horizon, bathing the land in sudden dark. A million insects began their serenade while I held her, wishing I could keep her safe in this moment forever.

But the after didn't give a shit about what we wanted.

"When we get back to the farm, I'm gonna wash the dirt

from your skin," I told her, rocking us gently. "Then I'll find a private spot, a little place where we can escape."

Kate pulled back slightly, brushing hair from her face. "You just want to use my body."

"Oh, hell yeah," I agreed, shifting her until I could palm her ass. "But I'm also selfish as fuck and want you to myself. No distractions. No, Audrey. No bastards."

She sighed, leaning back into me. "That sounds wonderful."

The night turned cold, the warmth of the day giving way to a chill in the air. Darkness came quick, no light but that from the waning moon and the pinprick stars.

That was one thing I didn't miss from the before. The quiet and utter brilliance of an uninterrupted night couldn't be beaten. I knew some struggled, fear of the dark and unknown overwhelming. But I was a creature of the night. I'd lived for far too long in shadowed corners, operating in darkness had become second nature.

Darkness didn't frighten me. Sunshine did. It was in the light that all your flaws became clear.

Butcher approached, a pack slung over his shoulder. "We're ready."

I nodded, disentangling myself from Kate. "Let's do this."

Armed to the teeth with guns, ammunition, and knives, we crept through the town avoiding bastard dens, and the odd kangaroo.

Texas peeled off, heading down to the lake to set up our decoy.

As we approached the hospital, I called a halt to our crew, assessing the options.

The hospital was typical of small-town Australia. It looked more like a converted single storey house. The grounds were surrounded by bush and scrub, the roads worn. There were limited options for cover if we came at it head-on. Instead, we'd need to split the team, moving through the back of the property and around the sides to set up Jo and Kate, before finding a decent entry point for the rest of us.

"Okay," I whispered with a nod. "Lights on in the left side of the hospital. Kate, you, and I will try for that side. The rest of you head along the right and get set up. When we hear the explosion, that's when we'll be good to go."

There were nods, faces grim but determined.

"Priority is Zero and antibiotics. Shoot first, ask later. Don't be a hero. We're in and out. If you get lost, get back to the cars and stay there. If anyone isn't back in an hour just leave. Any questions?"

There were head shakes.

"Right, move out."

Chapter Twenty-Five

Kate

Wrath boosted me onto the water tank, the only sound the scraping of my feet against the side, and the flapping of worn flags in the cold breeze.

He watched me get into position, his face grim. I shot him a smile and a thumbs up, then set up, laying down on my belly, positioning the sniper rifle he'd given me. Ava had long ago become the little voice in my head that prompted me to do all the final checks.

Snipers in the army trained for years for perfection. They could lie for days, watching and waiting for that perfect moment.

I was an average shot who just needed to get lucky enough times to help her friends. My role wasn't to take individuals out, it was to provide my team with enough time to get themselves safe—anything more was a bonus.

The discussion I'd had with Audrey about murder ran through my head. Referring to killing or wounding someone as a bonus felt wrong, shameful, criminal. But I needed to put that aside and allow that in the after this was war and bad people, truly evil individuals, had to die.

Wrath squeezed my leg and I looked down, sending him an air kiss.

He rolled his eyes but grinned, his teeth flashing in the dim light of the moon. With that final exchange, he faded into the shadows.

I sucked in a deep breath, holding it for a moment before slowly exhaling.

Clear mind, calm heart, steady hands.

I repeated the mantra Ava had drilled into Jo and me over many long months. She'd forced us to practice at all hours of the day and night, keeping us awake for days in order to train our bodies to respond to stress.

A light switched on in one of the windows and I braced, watching for movement.

A man appeared a moment later, his face shadowed. He was speaking to someone I couldn't see.

Audrey stepped out of the shadows, her face serene as she started for the door of the hospital.

Here we go.

I watched as she moved around, coming into the light. The man in the window caught sight of her, his body shooting upright before he disappeared.

Please God, I know we don't have a chummy relationship, but if you could see fit to keep Audrey safe, I'd be awfully thankful.

I watched through the scope as the door burst open, two men tumbling outside, guns pointed at Audrey.

"Hands up!" one of them barked, light spilling out from the hospital to send long shadows across the yard.

Audrey stuck her hands up, a waiver in her voice. "I'm so sorry! I saw your light and was hoping you might be a safe haven. My family were eaten by zombies outside town. I managed to escape but…."

She began to sob, loud and uncontrollably as the men exchanged glances.

"Well, come in then. I'm sure we can find you a little place to curl up."

"Oh, thank you!" Audrey rushed for the guy, wrapping her arms around him in an exuberant hug. "Thank you so much! My heroes!"

"Yeah well… don't thank us just yet." I heard the second guy mutter as they escorted her inside.

The door shut behind them, leaving us to wait. The night stretched, no unusual sounds coming from inside the hospital. Mosquitos buzzed around my ears, bugs crawling over my body as I stared down the scope, completely focussed on the yard.

Come on Texas. Any time now.

As if to answer my unspoken direction, a flash lit the yard, blinding me. I blinked, the imprint of the flash dancing, as a mushroom cloud ballooned up, lit by the raging explosion below. A heartbeat later, a shockwave hit me like a punch to the face, sliding me back on the water tank. Windows shattered, dirt, leaves, rocks, and other debris raining down as whatever discarded equipment that had been laying around the yard went flying.

In the aftermath, I scrambled back into position, shaking my head, and blinking rapidly to clear my vision. I heard a car alarm wailing in the distance, screams and shouts coming from inside the now windowless hospital.

Jesus, Texas. What did you do?

Men spilled out of the hospital, guns in hand. I watched as

women tried to follow, a child screaming on the hip of one, blood dripping down his little face.

"Get those bitches back inside!" barked a man in faded camo.

I marked him, waiting for my shot.

Two men turned back to the women, pointing guns at their heads, herding them inside.

"What was it?" one man asked as they all stared at the mushroom cloud.

"Coming from the lake," another said, pinching the bridge of his bleeding nose. "Reckon it blew?"

The guy in the faded military fatigues shrugged. "Maybe. Could be an animal got brave enough to head out that way and tripped something."

"Told you we shouldn't have killed them on the platform. That fuel could have kept us moving for weeks."

They were quiet for a moment, all staring at the orange glow coming from the lake.

"Either way, an explosion like that is gonna have every bastard for miles heading this way."

"Orders?"

I waited, listening.

"Go get the slaves. We need to move."

A reflection flickered my way from the far side of the yard, followed immediately by another. I didn't move, just waited, knowing the signal would come.

Men began to stream out of the hospital carrying boxes and bags, arms loaded with weapons, food, and medical equipment. A woman in dirty jeans and a filthy white shirt followed, trying to halt the movement of one man.

"Please, just leave us here. We'll only slow you down."

He shook her off, continuing to walk towards the carpark

where men were opening trucks, readying them to take the supplies.

And humans.

I counted twenty-three men, plus the boss who stood in the middle of the yard, directing the flow.

Twenty-four isn't great odds.

I didn't move, simply plotted potential trajectories that would allow me to hit as many as possible in the shortest time available.

As I watched, a man forced two women from the house. Both carried children, pushing them down the path towards the waiting trucks. One stumbled, the man immediately jerking her upright, slapping her across the face.

My fingers itched to pull the trigger, taking him out.

Clear mind, calm heart, steady hands... then kill the bastards.

They made it halfway across the yard before the reflected light flashed again.

One. Two. Three.

I pulled the trigger, taking out the boss. He went down part of his head nothing more than mist and bone fragments now covering the dirt yard.

I immediately shifted, using the shock and confusion to take out another two, one was the man who'd slapped the woman, another who'd reached for his gun.

Clear mind, calm heart, steady hands. Shoot to kill.

Every one of Ava's directions came back to me as I laid down fire, taking out enough men in the confusion to improve our odds.

The women were racing back to the hospital, heading for safety. I tried to clear a path, Jo assisting. Pope, Wrath and Butcher burst onto the scene. In a dance of blood and fury, they charged through the men, shooting and stabbing, punching, and kicking, violence and cold vengeance.

I watched as Wrath swept his leg out, tripping a retreating man. In the same instance the guy went down, another tried to punch Wrath. He ducked, stabbing the guy in the throat, blood spraying as he jerked the knife free, then twisted firing his gun, the man on the ground jerking once before slumping onto his stomach, blood oozing from his chest.

Wrath personified.

The firestorm of bullets slowed, Wrath, Butcher and Pope meticulous and coordinated. Their movements an almost hypnotic dance of grim determination and unleashed brutality.

Jo's bullet caught the last one in the yard as he turned, attempting to flee.

A quick sweep showed nothing but bodies.

"Cover us," Wrath yelled to Jo and me as the men moved to the door. "Watch for bastards."

Texas materialised on the far corner of the building. "Less than three minutes until they head this way. The explosion knocked out the gate holding them at the fairgrounds."

Wrath nodded, replacing the magazine of his gun. "Change of plans. Texas, Pope, get the trucks ready. We move, we move quick."

The two men peeled off, heading for the carpark and the idling trucks, leaving Jo and me to watch over the yard.

"On three," Wrath instructed.

"One." His boot hit the door, sending it back with a crash. He'd told me earlier he did this because it took anyone listening by surprise.

The men surged through the door, the sounds of screams and cries coming from inside the hospital. I saw flashes from the window, figures lit for a moment before disappearing.

Clear mind, calm heart, steady hands.

A man flew through the broken window, taking out the remaining glass. I hit him with one to the chest. A guy tried to run from the side door, Jo fired before I could get a hit, taking him down with one to the leg and another to his neck.

In the distance, I could hear the growls and cries. Butcher and Pope were frantically carrying the supplies from yard to truck, ensuring we didn't leave anything of value behind.

Hurry, Wrath.

The sounds of gunfire quietened, leaving a vacuum of uncertainty.

Please be alright.

A shadow crossed the doorway before exiting, Audrey waving towards Jo.

"Stand down! We won!" she yelled, gesturing back at the hospital. "Hurry! We need help."

I packed up the gun, emptying the chamber and flicking the safety before popping it back in its carry bag. I tossed it to the ground and followed, dropping with an oof as I hit.

"You right?" Audrey asked, tilting her head my way.

"Uh-huh." I picked up the gun, slinging it over my shoulder. "Lead on."

Inside the hospital was a blood bath. Men in fatigues littered the halls like broken dolls, their blood painting the linoleum floor in a sea of liquid red.

"The women were held in the main room, the men they hadn't yet killed are in the back. Pope and Wrath are down there. We found one of the doctors, she's rallying the women. By my calculations, we only have a few minutes to raid this place before the bastards arrive."

Outside there was a gunshot, followed quickly by another.

"Or my calculations could be wrong," Audrey corrected, picking up her speed. "Come on!"

We ran down a hall, finding a small contingent of women rushing about. Two teenagers corralled the younger children, while the rest stuffed pillowcases, boxes, and bound bedspreads with medical equipment.

"Medications?" Audrey asked an older woman in the middle of the room.

"Down the hall. Desi's already there packing."

Another gunshot sounded outside followed by a bellow from Texas.

"They're coming!"

"Audrey, take them to the trucks," Jo ordered, turning for the door. "We'll get the meds."

We ran down the hall, skidding to a stop next to the nurses' office where a woman was scooping armfuls of medication into a pillowcase.

"Here." I dropped my gun, opening the duffle bag. I lifted it, sweeping my arm across a shelf sending bottles and boxes of medication dropping into the bag. "What's essential?"

"Everything!" the woman snapped back, frantically snatching at a stray bottle.

"Antibiotics? Fluids?" Jo asked, looking around.

"In that," the woman said as she nodded at a large medical fridge. "But they need to remain cold."

"Move!" Butcher strode in, Pope on his tail. He checked the fridge contents, latched the lock then ripped the cords from the wall, nodding at Pope. "Got it."

Together they heaved the fridge out of the door, scraping and shoving as they manoeuvred it outside.

Bastards were running down the street towards the waiting truck, Texas and some of the rescued women desperately trying to pick them off.

"Is that everyone?" I asked, dragging my bag with me. "Where's Wrath?"

"No time." Butcher and Pope heaved the fridge into the back of the truck, the rest of us attempting to lend a hand. We got it loaded as the first bastard made it to the edge of the carpark.

Jo spun, pulling a pistol from Butcher's jeans and firing, hitting the animal in the head.

"Good shot," Texas called, still firing. "Everyone in the trucks! We gotta go!"

I looked around, my heart pounding as the main surge of the horde began their run across the field. "Where's Wrath?"

"Kate, we gotta go." Audrey tugged at my arm urgently, trying to pull me up and into the truck bed as women and children climbed around me, scrambling to get in. "Kate!"

"Wrath!" I screamed as the truck began to move. "Wrath!"

Texas abandoned his post, sprinting for the truck. He scooped me up, throwing me into the bed before jumping up behind me. He got in as the first bastard wave hit, their hands scratching at his legs.

"Fuck!" He kicked out, clocking one in the head. It fell, tripping those behind it. Another growled, clawing at the truck. Jo stood, legs shoulder-width apart, her big eyes wild, hair standing on end, fired, dropping it with one hit.

"Oh m-m-my God, o-o-oh my G-G-God," I muttered over and over, rocking as the truck picked up speed, leaving the horde and the now overrun hospital behind.

Audrey pulled me into her arms, holding me tight.

"He'll be fine," she assured me in a hoarse whisper. "He'll

meet us at the rendezvous."

Jo collapsed beside us, her hand reaching out to grip mine. "Pope's driving the other truck. Butcher's got this one. Texas is…." She gestured at the man who was being stripped of his pants by the doctor. "Causing a fuss."

She squeezed my hand, her palm clammy. "We survived, Kate. Wrath will as well."

Around us, women and children sobbed alternatively wailing and thanking us. The truck bumped along the silent roads, creaking and groaning under us as bottles of pills rolled across the floor, unsecured in the scramble to leave.

And all the while I quietly died inside as we watched the town fade into darkness.

Chapter Twenty-Six

Kate

"No!" I stomped my foot, glaring at Butcher. "I'm not going."

He ran a hand through his hair. Lines that hadn't been there before tonight were carved into the planes and grooves of his face. He looked like a man grieving.

"He'll be here," I said, my voice catching. "H-h-he p-p-promised m-me."

Wrath was late. We'd stopped at the rendezvous point, taking stock. Texas had been lucky, avoiding both scratches and bites from the bastards. The rescued women and children were in various stages of shock. I knew we needed to get them to safety. I knew we had to get the medicine to Zero.

But my heart rejected everything but Wrath.

"Kate," Butcher swallowed. "We'll leave one of the cars. If he gets out—"

"W-w-when," I corrected, hugging myself tight.

"When," he acquiesced. "He'll come here and be able to drive himself home. But we can't stay here. We need to get these people to safety. And you promised—we all did. No heroes, remember? If anyone wasn't back in an hour Wrath told us to leave."

Every molecule of my body protested that direction. I wanted to rage. Scream. Lash out. I wanted to burn the town to the ground to find him.

Instead, I sucked in a breath, shaking my head. "I-I-I'll s-stay here."

Butcher sighed. "You know I can't let you do that. Wrath would kill me."

Tears burned at the back of my eyes, threatening to spill over. "Please...."

"No," his voice broke, his arms reaching to pull me into his chest. "I'm sorry, Kate. So, fucking sorry. But I need to honour his wishes. Wrath would want you safe. Let me make you safe."

I bit the inside of my cheek, the metallic taste of blood hitting my tongue.

Don't you dare cry. He's not dead.

I had to believe that. I had to.

I nodded, stepping back, straightening my shoulders to stare at Butcher. "F-f-fine. B-b-but you have to e-ex-ex-explain why there'll b-b-be no ho-ho-h-hot water when he gets h-h-home."

Butcher nodded, not quite hiding the grief in his eyes. "Promise."

I turned, heading to the SUV we'd be leaving behind. Inside I found a notepad and pen. Quickly I scribbled a note just for Wrath. I pressed a kiss to the paper, folding it then tucked it under the windscreen wiper.

Come back to me. I'm waiting.

With a final glance at the town in the distance, I pivoted, walking to one of the trucks and climbing in.

A woman shifted, letting me settle beside her. The truck started under us, the vibrations rattling through our bodies.

"Do you think the others survived?" she whispered, her gaze on the town in the distance. "The men, I mean. I know the rest of the town is lost."

"Yes," I answered honestly. "And they'll come find us."

She nodded. "I hope so."

The truck lurched forward and then found its rhythm, bumping along the deserted road, leaving behind the horde, the town, and Wrath.

Chapter Twenty-Seven

Wrath

I could hear the motherfucking horde bearing down on us.

"Come on," I ordered, slicing the cable ties off the last man in the room. "We gotta go."

"Where?" one of the men asked, rubbing his hands. "There's nowhere to go."

"Up, we'll hide on the roof."

They exchanged glances but I didn't have time to argue. They could either follow me or die. I'd done my duty.

I pulled my one remaining gun free, checking the safety was off.

On three.

One—

I kicked open the door, gun up, eyes scanning.

"Clear, let's go."

We hurried through the hospital, headed for the back entrance. Most of the men were able to walk, though they had various broken bones, contusions, and bruising. Except for one guy, who looked more like mincemeat than human. Unlike the women I'd seen as I'd shot the place up, these guys had been treated to a pounding.

I paused at the exit, glancing around. A solitary bastard prowled across the yard, following the dim lights of the trucks in the distance. I held up a finger to my lips, gesturing at them to freeze. I crept outside, looking around as the bastard took off, disappearing into the darkness.

I moved to the rail that ran along a deck, lifting onto it and twisting to reach for the roof. With a grunt, I heaved myself up. I lay flat, pulling myself forward and tilting until I could peer down to the doorway.

"Alright, quick now. Let's lift your mate up first then we can get the rest of you up."

A man scrambled up beside me, three men on the ground lifting their friend until we could reach his arms, hauling him up and dragging him across the roof to a safe spot. He moaned briefly before passing out.

"Stay with him," I ordered, pulling a water canister from my backpack. "And get him to drink some water. It won't take the pain away but it might keep him alive 'til morning."

Once the men were up, we camped on the roof, watching, and listening as the bastards ran through the hospital searching for us.

"What happened on the lake?" I asked quietly as the bastard horde began to move back towards the fire, likely drawn by the occasional explosion.

"About three weeks ago a caravan came into town," the older guy next to me started, his gaze fixed on the glow from the fire. He'd introduced himself as John, an elder of the local mob.

"We'd been living for the last year on the lake. We'd made it through winter in decent shape. We'd only lost one of the old-timers to pneumonia. Life was…." He trailed off, shaking his head. "Not good. But not bad. You know? It's the after. Life is life. And we're living it. We were content."

Around him, the other eight men nodded, all with grief written into the grooves of their faces.

"The caravan somehow wrangled half the horde down into the showgrounds. Meant that, if we were smart, we could set off distractions at one end of town and go for raids on the other."

I smacked at a mosquito sucking at my arm. "You chose to stay on the lake?"

They nodded.

"Safer," the narrator told me. "We could hear people coming and no bastard can get out that far."

I thought of the drowning bastards we'd escaped from. "Smart."

"Then the caravan rolled in and we celebrated their victory." His voice broke and he looked away, staring out into the night.

"They poisoned us," a young man said from across the roof. "Some kind of sleeping drug. When we woke, half of us were dead."

"And the rest?"

"Enslaved."

I nodded, digging in my bag for protein bars. "When did they move you to the hospital?"

"Three days ago. We'd been living on the platform with… with the bodies. Their boss finally had enough of the smell and decided to move us. The hospital seemed the best option—quick escape if shit went bad."

"Not to mention a few of them like to shoot up the morphine," another man muttered.

I found the small bag of protein bars, pulling it free and

handing it around the group. The men gratefully accepted.

"You know where they're from? Who they're affiliated with?"

The younger guy shook his head, ripping open the protein wrapper with his teeth. "Militia group, no idea where they're from, they made mention of a few places but nowhere specific. From the shit we overheard, looks like slavers are wanting people for farms and ships. We've heard whispers that some of the bigger organisations are looking for cheap, disposable labour to work in the mines and oil fields. They wanna get business back on track."

I blew out a breath, shaking my head. "Who would have thought the world would end and big business is still tryna make a buck. Capitalism, am I right?"

The mood lightened as shadow smiles touched the faces of these beaten men.

I nodded towards the glow. "Sorry about your people. When we came up with the idea for the distraction, one of our members felt strongly that we should give them the best burial we could manage. We should have looked for a second option."

"No, this is good. We couldn't bury them anyway."

We fell silent, watching the fire slowly dim.

"You wanna say a few words?" I asked the group.

All heads turned to the man beside me. He swallowed, nodding, tears shining in the dim light.

After a long, silent moment he pressed a hand to his heart, the rest of us doing the same.

"To those we left behind," he began, his voice cracking with emotion. "You were the best of us, just as we are the best of you. Our families, our friends, our people. Together we were one. Now we are less. We are less without you. Our world is less. Our days are dimmer, our nights colder." He sucked in a shuddering breath.

"I can't give you the rites of my people. I can't honour you in the tradition of our ancestors. But I can remember you. I can remember your faces, your stories, your words. And I will. We will."

He broke off, switching to his mother language, the language of one of the local mobs. With tears streaming down his face, he sang softly in the language of his ancestors, inviting us into his grief, inviting the community of men around me to share in the grief of their loss.

A second man joined in, his voice also soft, both mindful of the bastards still prowling the grounds.

As I sat there, listening to the song that sounded as if plucked from the darkest part of their soul, I thought of Kate. Kate's grin, her stutter, her eyes, her lips, her hands. I thought of the dirt under her fingernails, of the gentle care with which she treated plants. I thought of her humour, her intelligence, I thought of her as a teenager, a young adult, now.

And I ached. I ached to hold her in my arms tonight, under this sad moon, while a community mourned for their loved ones.

The song ended and silence fell, the men in various stages of open mourning. Some cried, some prayed, others sat stony-eyed, looking off to the fire.

We stayed like that until the sun began to rise, the first rays of the morning tickling the horizon, painting the sky with a blush of colour.

The singer broke our silence. "A new day dawns, stranger. Tell us, where are we headed?"

I blew out a breath, the weight of their safety heavy on my shoulders. "To a safe haven, if you'll come."

The man looked around the group, meeting the eyes of every member before returning to me. "We will."

I nodded, gesturing out at the yard still filled with enough bastards to make things interesting. "Now to just get past these guys."

The younger man leaned forward, a chunk of thick hair falling across his brow. "Actually, I might have a solution to that."

Chapter Twenty-Eight

Wrath

"Dude, this is either batshit crazy or fucking brilliant, I'm not sure," I told the young guy as we crept through the hospital halls. He'd introduced himself as King, and I had to assume it'd been his name in the before because every man on that roof called him by it.

"Let's go with brilliant," King replied, switching his knife between his hands.

A bastard prowled down the opposite hall, hissing and spitting. We froze, not a breath of movement between us. The former man continued, a damaged foot dragging against the floor, hands curved into those horrible twisted claws.

"Close," King breathed next to me. "It's this way."

He led me down a hall, through a second corridor and into a training room, shutting the door behind us.

"Well this is creepy as fuck," I commented looking around the room.

The room looked like any other hospital ward, complete with beds, equipment and mannequins tucked neatly into dusty beds.

"But useful." King pointed at the mannequin in the closest bed. "You grab that one."

I picked it up, grunting in surprise at its weight.

"Well, John Doe here could lose a few pounds," I said, hefting it up and over my shoulder.

"Yeah, they're meant to mimic the actual weight of a dead person."

I looked around. "Anything else we need?"

"Nope, we can raid the rest on the way out," King said, sheathing his knife.

"Great, now to just get back."

Carrying the dolls in a fireman hold, we crept back through the halls to a cool room at the back of the hospital complex.

"In here," King said, pushing the door open with his hip.

Inside, we dropped the mannequins to the floor and began to pull open fridges and freezers.

"What is this?" I asked, holding up some vials filled with clear liquid.

King shrugged, pulling open another freezer. "Probably medication or some shit. You can take some if you want, but it ain't gonna last long outside a cool room."

I looked around, throwing open a couple of cupboards. In one, tucked in the back, dusty from neglect, was one of those cooler containers they used to transport organs. I pulled it free, finding some ice packs in one of the freezers.

"How are these still on?"

King pointed up at the roof. "Solar. There's a local solar farm just outside town. As part of the deal to build it, they had to have a steady supply pushing to the essential services in town. The people left, the sun didn't. Hence, the power is still chugging along."

I lined the bottom and sides with ice packs then snatched handfuls of vials, shoving them into the container, trying to grab different types, cursing my fucking ignorance.

Kate's voice whispered in my mind, calming my actions.

Anything we recover is a win, Wrath. The most important thing is that you come back to me.

I'm coming, Kate. Don't you doubt that.

I clipped the cooler shut then shoved it in my pack. The pack was bulky on my back, hanging awkwardly.

"Here, found the blood." King tossed me the packets from a fridge.

"Are these still good?" I asked, holding the packet up to the light.

"Probably not. Blood only lasts 42 days. But like everything else in the after, they'll do."

He pulled a knife from his boot, dropping down to carve through the chest of the training mannequin. I did the same, pulling the flimsy silicon apart. Together, we packed the inside with the blood packets.

"This is gonna be a bitch to carry," King muttered as we roughly bound the chests back together.

"When in life isn't it?"

I helped him pick the damn thing up, settling it across his shoulders. "You good?"

"Yeah, let's do this."

I followed him, carrying mine behind. We hurried through the halls; our footsteps heavy under the weight.

"Left up here then—"

A bastard appeared from one of the rooms, snarling and growling, spit flying as it ran at us.

"Fuck!"

I dropped the weight spinning to give it my back, using my overloaded pack as a buffer as I pulled the knife from my hip.

Bullets bring bastards. Take him down quiet.

I rammed him back, pinning him between the wall and my pack, tossing the knife to King.

"Kill it!"

He caught the knife, immediately advancing to stab it over my shoulder. I heard the crunch, the crack of bone as the knife found its mark. The bastard fell quiet, the struggling at my back ceasing.

I stepped away from the wall, King doing the same. We looked down, a knife sticking out of the bastard's eye.

"Good aim."

King grinned. "Not much I'm good at but killing bastards? I'm fucking amazing."

Noises from the far end of the hall had us both scrambling. We needed to get out. Now.

Heaving the mannequins, we made it to the back of the hospital where men stood at the ready, helping to heave the heavy bitches up onto the roof. We scrambled up as the first bastards came through the doors, following us.

"Ready?" I asked, looking to Paul, a miner who'd become stranded in the town after the world ended.

He lifted two small devices, handing them over. "They're rough but they'll get the job done."

King and I took one each, placing it into a small space we'd left in the mannequins, sealing them up completely.

"Let's just hope they're attracted to the blood," King muttered, tying off his stitch.

"We ready?" Paul asked.

I looked to King who nodded.

"Yep, let's get this party started."

The men began hollering, yelling, and screaming, calling over every bastard within earshot. My body tensed as the bastards crowded into the yard, hissing and snarling, growling as they shifted around, trying to figure out a way up to us.

"Fuck this better work," King yelled, heaving up one of the mannequins.

"Ready?" I asked, taking its legs.

"Yep, on three." We swung it, back then forth, counting, "One, two, three!"

On three, we sent it flying into the gathered horde. Immediately the bastards scattered, avoiding the flying projectile. The mannequin landed with a sickening thump, legs and arms splayed at broken angles.

The second mannequin followed a moment later, landing on the other side of the yard.

"Take cover!"

We hit the deck, arms protecting heads.

One. Two. Three. Four. Five. Si-

A wave of heat hit us, searing hair, and skin. A wall of sound hit next, my ears popping with the pressure. I looked up as droplets of wet rained down on us, the world now a quiet, high pitched ringing.

Bastard Blood. Fuck!

I pushed that worry aside, leaping to my feet, helping the men around me as we began to scramble, climbing off the roof and heading for the road.

I could feel my voice leaving my throat, feel the rough scrape of it as I bellowed directions at the men. But my hearing was shot, nothing but a high-pitched ringing in my ears.

Supporting each other, helping the weak, we rushed down

the main road, headed for the outskirts of town.

My hearing came back around a kilometre down the road, the faint high-pitched ringing persisting.

"Which way?" King yelled, making exaggerated gestures.

"Hearing's back," I told him as I pointed to the right. "This way."

They followed me down to the entrance of the town, half dragging, half carrying their wounded. The few bastards that roamed the road were quickly dispatched; the men determined to survive.

I breathed a sigh of relief when I saw the SUV parked by the faded sign welcoming us to the lake.

Get to the vehicle. Get clean. Get to Kate.

I repeated my checklist silently, rapidly readjusting my plan as I considered our options.

There were ten of us. It'd be a tight fit, but beggars couldn't be choosers.

"I'll drive. King, help load the injured in the back."

I climbed in, slamming the door, and finding the keys hidden under the driver's seat.

Thank you, Texas.

The car doors slammed, King jumping in the passenger seat. "We're good. Let's motor."

Ahead, bastards began to emerge from the scrub, features twisted by the disease into a grotesque parody of humanity.

"Hold on!"

I floored the vehicle, grunting as we ploughed through the horde. Bodies flew across the bonnet, the SUV bumping as it crunched over bodies with sickening ease.

Kill or be killed. Them or you.

We cleared the small horde, motoring down the road, leaving

the horrors of Lake Cargelligo behind.

A few kilometres into the journey, as safety seemed within our grasp, King blew out a long breath.

"So, circling back—I'd say that turned out to be a fucking brilliant idea."

I raised an eyebrow, my lip twitching as I glanced at King. The young guy grinned, chuckling.

"You know, if you find Farmer's place isn't for you, Nameless Souls would take you on."

He sobered, his eyebrows lifting. "I'll… keep it in mind. Thanks."

With a nod, I looked back to the road, my foot pressing on the accelerator, picking up our speed. Kate was waiting for me.

Chapter Twenty-Nine

Kate

Long shadows stretched across the compound yard, the sun hanging low in the clear sky. Dirt coated my hands, a familiar comfort that eased my anxiety for a moment.

"Kate? You in here?" Audrey called from the entry to the greenhouse.

"Over by the tomatoes."

There were mumbles as she navigated through the rows. I heard her wondering aloud how she was meant to know what a tomato plant looked like.

On an ordinary day that would have made me laugh. Today, it felt like I would never smile again.

The dog found me first, snuffling under my arm to give me a cheeky lick on my chin before leaping into the garden and rolling in the freshly tilled soil. The little animal had become Audrey's shadow, following her around the farm.

"Oh, Killer! No!" Audrey cried, reaching for the dog. "You just had a bath."

The strangely named Killer wiggled in delight, covering himself in the thick dirt. Audrey sighed, dropping down beside me. "Do you know anything about training animals? I've never owned a pet before, and Farmer's bookshelf is woefully under-resourced in dog training manuals."

I wanted to smile. I wanted to so badly. But the deep ache that dwelled in my soul prevented me from feeling any emotions but life-altering anxiety.

"Have you asked Lottie?"

Audrey waved her hands. "She said to figure it out. She's busy splitting time between helping with Zero and the other injured and looking after the farm animals." Audrey looked pointedly at Killer, who'd finished rolling, and now lay panting happily in the soil. "She acts as if this isn't an emergency. I mean, are dogs normally this attracted to dirt?"

I shrugged, reaching over to give Killer a pat then gently ease him out of the garden.

Audrey watched as I scooped gravel from a bag beside me, tipping it into the hole left by Killer.

"What are you doing?" she asked, watching as I folded the gravel into the loose mix.

"Making it less wet." I scooped again, adding more. "We can't improve the condensation by much—not until Farmer makes the improvements to the greenhouse. So instead, I'm improving the soil moisture levels."

"And gravel helps?"

"Yep."

Audrey silently watched as I repeated the process, the routine motion only slightly calming the storm inside.

"He'll be back," Audrey said after I reached the end of the first garden.

"I know."

I moved to stand but she halted me with a hand to my arm. I

looked up, finding her solemn gaze on me.

"He loves you, Kate. When I first started my scenario research, I explored networks. People. I looked at what survivors did and said that motivated them to survive."

She let go of my arm, resting her hand on Killer's head. "For some, it was duty or honour. For others, experience, and training. But for a select few, the ones who triumphed against the toughest of odds, it was what I called the human factor."

I tilted my head to the side, encouraging her to continue.

"Data can't lie. Humans can, humans *do*, but data can't. And what the data told me about that final group? The ones who I couldn't find any rational explanation for how they beat the odds? I found it in the psych interviews." She shook her head, a wry smile on her face. "Love, longing and belonging. And occasionally sheer dumb luck. But mostly, love. When we looked at the data, when I examined every touchpoint, people were driven by it. By love of country or home. By love of family or self. Love came into every decision, every determination, every point."

She chuckled; the sound amused but sad. "I rejected that data so thoroughly that I made the decision to recruit women unencumbered by such a vulnerable emotion. No partners, no children, no strong family ties." She shook her head. "That lasted for all of ten minutes once I decided I needed Blair and Ellie. But even the sisters we recruited had to serve a purpose. Jo, Beth, and Ruby had ties to each other but not their extended family. Ava and Lottie were approved only because they had skills I needed."

Audrey looked at me, shoving her glasses up her nose, her face determined but fearful. "Love is an unknown variable I can't account for. It makes people act in irrational ways. And that terrifies me." She reached out, brushing a tear I hadn't even realised I'd shed from my cheek. She examined the wet on her finger, staring at it as if it held answers.

"It terrifies… and delights. It gives me hope where before I had nothing but determination." She dropped her hand, wiping it against her jeans. "Determination will get you far. We survived on determination for the first few months. But when shit got scary, when we got attacked that first time, determination wasn't enough. Hope—that's what kept us going."

She pushed to her feet, briskly dusting off her jeans. "Anyway, what I'm saying is, don't be surprised if Wrath comes running through those doors demanding to kiss you before dinner tonight."

"I don't know, I'm pretty hungry."

Audrey and I both jolted, twisting toward the far end of the aisle, Killer scrambling to his feet and letting out a surprised bark.

Blood and dirt caked his skin, his hair a mess of dust and sweat. A bruise marked one cheek; a cut oozed slowly on his arm. Dark circles and bloodshot eyes, worn clothes, and, as always, that fucking backpack.

Wrath had never looked more alive, more beautiful, more whole than in that moment.

I shoved to my feet, sprinting toward him. He met me halfway, lifting me up, spinning me round, his lips on mine.

"When?" I asked between wet, hungry, demanding kisses. "How?"

"Now. And it's a long story," he answered, his fingers delving into my hair to hold my head still while he fucked my mouth with his.

I gave in, needing him, surrendering to this grateful, joyous, wonderful relief.

"I'm uh… I'll see you two later."

Dimly, I heard Audrey and Killer leave, the door on the greenhouse closing behind them. I pulled back, touching the blood on his face.

"Bastard?"

He shook his head. "We're clean. This is from a stupid branch that caught me square in the face." He slid me down his body, bending so I could see the cut just above his hairline. "I'd have been here sooner, but the damned SUV blew a tyre ten kilometres out. We had to haul arse to get here."

I pulled his face down, peppering him with kisses. "I love you. I love you. Fuck, I love you."

He grinned, capturing my lips, his fingers playing with the skin at my hip. "You need me to wash or…?"

In answer, I surged forward, gripping him tight. The slow slide of his tongue against mine sent me spinning, my body a needful beast. Wrath's hands lifted my shirt, his fingers grazing up my skin as he pushed it up, bunching it below my breasts.

I caught his lip between my teeth, nipping him as he unclasped my bra. His answering groan could have been heard all the way back to Lake Cargelligo.

"Missed you," I whispered, as Wrath nibbled his way down my neck. "Don't do that to me again, okay?"

He pulled back, just far enough to force me to lift my arms as he pulled my shirt off, tossing it aside.

"Can't promise that," he told me, his hands coming up to cup my breasts. "But I promise, on my life, that I'll fight with every part of my being to get back to you."

I shivered, tilting my head back, granting him access to my

collarbone. He kissed his way down to my breasts. Wrath jerked my bra down my arms, tossing it aside. He cupped my breasts, lifting them to his lips as if I were a bountiful offering to a god.

The God of Wrath.

I nearly laughed, nearly told him that silly thought. But any levity fizzled the moment his mouth closed over my nipple.

"Wrath!"

He grinned, his mouth hot and wet. My hands dropped to his hips, anchoring myself.

"Wrath…," I panted.

"Mm?" He shifted his mouth to my left nipple, dragging his tongue over my skin before he grazed me with his teeth.

"You were saying?" he asked.

"I need you in me. I need us c-c-connected. Now!"

He pulled back, ripping his shirt over his head, and dropping it. Together, we fumbled, urgent fingers awkward as we unbuttoned pants and buckles, removed boots and socks, pulling and shoving until we were both naked.

I pushed Wrath to the ground, settling over his thighs. We froze for a moment, the last of the light bathing us in a warm glow.

"Kate…." My name sounded like a prayer coming from his lips.

"I love you," I told him, gripping his cock. "I vow to find my way back to you, or die trying."

He sat up, his arms wrapping tight around me, as his gaze met mine. His eyes were on fire—desire, want, and hunger raging in their depths.

"And I vow to find my way back to you, or die trying."

These were marriage vows, stronger and more binding

than any uttered within a church. Here, under the big sky, surrounded by plants, we promised love, life, and self.

We promised to be each other's after.

I shifted, sinking down onto his cock, both of us gasping as he filled me.

"Fuck… Kate…." I barely recognised Wrath's voice; it was so hoarse with need.

He shifted slightly, changing the angle, his cock pressing against the wonderfully sensitive spot inside me.

My body convulsed, my hips shifting as I began to ride him. His hands settled on my hips, his face twisted into pained pleasure.

"Gonna. Come," he panted through gritted teeth.

I picked up my pace but Wrath's hands halted me. Urgently he pressed me down, taking control. He thrust with power, lifting me, causing my breasts to bounce and my body to clench.

"Wrath!"

The sun set at the exact moment I came, darkness covering us as we both spiralled. He delved one hand into my hair, forcing my head down to meet his mouth. He feasted, devouring me hungrily, his cock continuing to thrust powerfully into my clenching pussy.

I cried out against his lips, one orgasm flowing into another. I felt him follow, his cum hot inside me, his cock pulsing and jerking, as he roared my name.

We collapsed, Wrath sprawled on the ground, me on his chest. The darkness embracing us like a welcome friend.

He is the monster in the dark. But I have nothing to fear from this God of Wrath.

As our skin cooled and our breathing slowed, Wrath's hands began to trail slowly up and down my back, his fingers gliding over skin, the warmth of him under me, utterly beguiling.

He pressed a kiss to my forehead, another to my cheek. And soon he was pressing kisses across my skin, heating us up once more.

"I love you," he chanted, thrusting into me. "Love you, Kate. I fucking love you."

I came once more, and then again. Our reunion ending when hunger drove us from the greenhouse.

We showered, Wrath lifting me against the tile, fucking me with raw abandon as water washed blood, dirt and sweat from our bodies.

Semi-presentable, we made it to the dining room, the team toasting Wrath's return. As we ate, the men he'd rescued told stories of his heroism, and recounted blow-by-blow action sequences.

"So you're a hero?" I asked, leaning against him as Farmer poured another round of whiskey into the gathered cups.

"Nah." He nuzzled my cheek, kissing the corner of my mouth. "Just desperate to get back to you."

I caught his hand, pulling him quietly from the room as the celebration continued late into the night.

We climbed the tower, finding our bed on the tall platform. We made love once again, under the light of the waning moon.

After, I lay in his arms, stroking his skin, my soul content to be here, in this moment, with him.

"Did you mean it?" Wrath asked, breaking the silence.

"Mean what?"

He cleared his throat. "Your vow."

I chuckled, snuggling in closer and pressing a kiss to his shoulder. "Oh yes."

He was silent for a moment. "Still want to marry you, Kate.

When we get to Cunnamulla, first thing we're gonna do. We'll get you a dress and a kutte, we'll stand in front of a preacher, and my brothers and your sisters will watch when I claim you."

Tears pricked my eyes but I refused to shed them. I'd waited my entire life for Wrath, and in one moment he'd handed me everything I'd ever desired.

"Is that a proposal?" I asked.

"Nah, it's a promise."

A smile broadened his lips, his eyes sparkled in the dark as he guided my face to his. "I love you, Sunshine."

"And I love you."

And in the moonlight, we made love that felt eternal.

Epilogue

Wrath

I slowed my bike, picking a path that looked to be the least bumpy. Kate's arms tightened around my middle, her body pressing closer as we hit unavoidable potholes.

We passed under a wooden archway. On it hung a sign that read *Nameless Souls Motorcycle Club – Cunnamulla Chapter*.

The gates in front of us opened, a prospect I recognised from previous visits, waving us through.

We parked in the middle of the yard, the convoy of trucks and vehicles finding their own spots.

I killed the engine, immediately twisting to steady Kate as she dismounted. She pulled her helmet free, her hair tumbling about her shoulders as she looked around.

"Well, this is…."

I laughed at her wide-eyed expression. "Our temporary home."

Everywhere you looked there were signs of people. The ranch had become a safe haven for our members, and, from the looks of it, traders and refugees.

"Are we safe?" Kate asked, leaning into me as I slung an arm around her shoulder.

"Always."

She allowed me to guide her inside, finding the vice president waiting to welcome us.

"The Prez is out on a hunt," he explained, shaking hands with each of our party. "But I'll send word. If you guys want to grab some chow and have a shower, our prospects can take you."

"Actually," I interrupted, pulling Kate closer. "You got a blacksmith around here?"

Kate looked up at me, her eyes shining with unshed tears, her lips pressed together.

"A blacksmith? What's he need a blacksmith for?" I heard Audrey ask, Jo immediately hushing her.

"Yeah, out back." The VP nodded at one of the prospects. "Take him to Smoke."

The kid escorted us out back to a large shed. Inside, a man beat hot iron, alternately cooling and heating until it formed the shape he wanted.

Smoke pushed up his helmet, looking from Kate to me.

"What can I do for you?"

I pulled a piece of paper from my back pocket, handing it over.

"Can you make that?" I dug in my pocket, pulling out a handful of necklaces and rings I'd collected over the years. "With this?"

The guy considered the drawing. "Yeah, I can probably make it work. Give me an hour or so."

"Great." I turned to the prospect. "You got a tailor around here?"

"That'd be old Beryl. Her hands are arthritic but she does the best stitches. Quick work too. Insists on making all the kuttes herself."

"Take us there."

In a dark little cabin that had been roughly shoved together, Beryl considered us through large, heavily magnified glasses.

"You'll be wanting a property patch," she said, nodding at Kate. "In addition to that dress."

Kate's breath caught, her gaze flying to me.

She stood in front of a mirror, dressed in a simple wedding gown. The old woman had taken one look at us and handed it over with a grin.

She'd never looked more beautiful.

I cleared my throat, adjusting my stance. "Yep. I got fuel, food or fabric. You can have whatever you want in exchange for it to be ready by tomorrow."

The old woman lifted her glasses, squinting at me.

"You young people, always thinking life is a trade." She looked at Kate. "Love is special. It doesn't get charged around here." She picked up a needle and began to thread it. "Come back tomorrow morning. I'll have it ready. And that dress too."

Outside, Kate pulled on my hand, digging her heels in.

"You okay?"

She shook her head, tears shimmering on her lashes. "You r-r-really m-me-meant it."

"Meant what, Sunshine?"

"T-t-that you w-wanted to marry me."

I chuckled, pulling her into my chest, my arms tight around her. "Of course."

We stood for a stolen moment together. The world around us might be utter chaos but with her, I always find my peace.

"Wrath?"

"Mm?"

"One day, when this is over, will you have a family with me?"

I gazed into her beautiful eyes; her face so fucking gorgeous it broke me every time. I thought of the big warehouse back down in Adaminaby. I thought of her women she'd left behind to go on this journey, and the bravery it took to take this leap of faith with me.

"In a heartbeat, Sunshine." I grinned, palming her ass. "But until then I think we'll need to put in a whole lot of practice. Gotta find just the right position to knock my woman up."

She laughed, the sound pure and true. It tumbled out of her, gliding across the air to embed on my soul.

Kate's words from weeks before echoed in my ears.

Obsession is consuming, containing, constraining. It doesn't allow for growth. Love follows you through all seasons of your life. Love is a journey; obsession is a cell.

I hadn't understood then, but it hit me now. Freedom, love was freedom.

"Love you, Sunshine."

She blinked up at me, her stunning face completely free from worry. "Let's go shower."

Roaring with laughter, I picked her up, throwing her over my shoulder in a fireman hold.

Love might be a journey, but Kate would always be my home.

And thank fuck for that.

***

Thank you so much for reading Wrath and Kate! The story continues with Ghost! I can't wait for you to read his story. The man is FILTHY!

I'm always looking for more people to join my ARC team. If you'd be interested, please fill out the form here.

Be sure to follow my Facebook page or check out my website for more information on the Nameless Souls series. Otherwise, keep reading for a little sneak peek!

Next in Series

Ghost | Book 3 Nameless Souls MC

Ava

Ghost exited the shower stall, coming out to stand behind me. I was still fucking with my stupid ass shoes.

"Ready?"

I looked up, about to make a sarcastic comment about these fucking heels when my gaze stuttered to halt on his crotch.

Dear fucking God.

He wore only three items of clothing—that fucking frat boy cap, grey sweat pants, and a sleeveless zip hoodie that he'd left open.

His insane eight pack with just the right amount of chest hair was fucking impressive but I'd seen that before. Nope, it was the outline of his cock against the grey material that killed me.

Oh God. Oh, my fucking God.

"Ava?"

I sucked in a breath, struggling and failing to lift my gaze from the impressive outline.

"Ava."

My name was no longer a question but a growl. As I watched, his impressive size lengthened, growing thicker, more rigid.

"Eyes," Ghost barked and I snapped, looking up.

He watched me, his face made from stone, but his eyes, oh his glorious eyes. They were hot and filled with filthy promises.

"I need to focus," he told me, his tone guttural. "Gotta win this."

I licked my lips, then bent, quickly tying the straps of the heel then straightened to a stand. The heels gave me a few extra inches that brought me closer to his height.

I reached out, sliding my hand down his chest, fingers running across his pecs and down his stomach, following the goody trail to the waistband of his sweats.

Ghost stood like a rock under my hand, motionless, craved from marble. Only the heat of his skin let me know he was a living, breathing man.

Well, that and his impressive dick.

My hand dropped further, cupping his cock through his sweats, the heavy weight hard and hot in my hand.

He growled, the rumble involuntary and delightfully animalistic. I ignored the flood of moisture that slicked my pussy at the sound.

Needing him to survive this battle, I placed my free hand on his shoulder, boosting myself up until my lips could brush his ear, my words only for him.

"Survive, and I might let you fuck my mouth. I know you've wanted it."

I pulled back but his hands shot out halting my retreat. One hand fisted my hair, the other pressing my hand back onto his thick cock, his body grinding against my palm.

I shuddered, wet heat drenching my underwear and thighs.

Ghost held me steady as he leaned in, his lips less than a hairs breadth from mine.

"And if I win? If I fuck those little boys up and win this fight? If I return your women will you give me your cunt, Ava? Will you let me taste your cream?"

My legs clenched, my nipples responding to the harsh need in his voice.

"You'd prefer that over a blow job even though you've tasted me before?" I asked, trying to sound casual even as I pressed closer, desperate to feel the rasp of my nipples against his chest.

His hand let go of mine, shifting to my hips, pulling me closer then coasting over my sides then down, lifting the hem of my skirt, his big, calloused hand slipping under to find my underwear, one finger rubbing against my mound.

"Soaked," he growled, his breath rough against my cheek. "You want this."

"Maybe."

His finger pulled my panties to the side, slipping between my lips to rub through my wet heat. I sucked in a breath at the intrusion. Blunt, rough and oh so fucking welcome, he rubbed my clit, teasing and stroking.

I shifted, swaying those two tiny breaths toward him, closing the distance between us, desperate and needing release.

It's been so long. Too fucking long.

Abruptly, Ghost pulled back, dropping his hands from my body, banking the heat in his eyes. I watched as he returned to that dead place inside him.

"Game time."

I took a second, reorientating myself. The heat from his touch still branded onto my skin. As I watched, he lifted his fingers to his mouth, licking my taste from them.

"You dirty fucker," I whispered, pressing my thighs together, hating and loving the way my body ached for him. "You better fucking win."

Fuck, Ava. Don't let him see how much you want this.

I straightened, fixing my skirt then stepping passed him, moving to lead us out of the locker room. I threw my parting words over my shoulder.

"Just saying, you better be fucking worth it."

Connect with Evie

Website
www.EvieMitchell.com

Instagram, Facebook and TikTok
@EvieMitchellAuthor

Facebook Group
Evie Mitchell's Greedy Reader Book Club

Books by Evie Mitchell

Nameless Souls MC Series
Runner
Wrath
Ghost

Elliot Security Series
Rough Edge
Bleeding Edge
Knife Edge

Capricorn Cove Series
Thunder Thighs
Double the D
Muffin Top
The Mrs. Clause
Beach Party
New Year Knew You
The Shake-Up
Double Breasted
As You Wish
You Sleigh Me
Resolution Revolution
Meat Load
Trunk Junk (Coming soon)

Archer Sibling Series
Just Joshing